NOT IN THE JOB DESCRIPTION

JESSIE ROBERTS

PROLOGUE

The screams don't even shake the pair skulking in the gloomy darkness outside the room their master uses for his hobby. They know what's going on in that chamber, and they do not care. It's not like this is something new. The master of the house knows they are out there. It doesn't bother him. Why would it? It's not like they will do anything to stop him, as if they even could.

A sound of bone breaking precedes the next blood-curdling scream echoing through the hall. "You chose wrong again!"

The black-haired woman glares at the blond man accusing her of not doing her job properly. "What do you want?! I can't see more than a picture until they are standing at the front door!"

The woman adjusts her black apron over the black dress she has to wear, ignoring another scream that issues from her latest failure's lungs. It's not that their employer is angry she chose wrong. He enjoys this too much.

Wiping his hands over his filthy coveralls, the man sighs. "I know he's happy either way, but peace would come if we can just find the right one."

"Peace," the woman scoffs, fixing the hair that fell out of place during the girl's struggle. No strand must be out of place. Her tight bun must be perfect. He hates disorder. She's already experienced what happens when he's displeased.

This time, they both flinch. That is a particularly shrill

scream. The woman glances at the door before turning her head back to her companion. "Do you really think we would ever have peace?"

Blond hair stands on end after he runs his hand through it, making the woman panic and quickly straighten it. He smacks her hand, annoyed by her attention, before straightening it himself. "You don't think he will? You know what he truly wants. He may not be able to end the *lives* of those in our village, but his rampage is still going to hurt."

"At least I won't have to clean *that* mess," she mumbles so quietly it's almost lost under the sounds coming from the room.

They are interrupted as the subject at hand bursts through the door, grinning with excitement and making his servants jump. "You know what to do," his raspy voice echoes in the quiet halls.

He is gone before they can answer, the click of his cane following his slow, yet animated, path. Entering the room, they take in the grisly scene without a single reaction. The dead woman's naked body is no longer recognizable. The simple, metal table holding the mangled flesh stands in the center of the once white room. The black-haired woman cannot understand why her master chose white for this room. This is going to be a tough mess to clean up.

Her companion brings in a dark tarp, even darker stains marring its shiny surface, and lays it next to the table. She doesn't understand why he never cleans the blood off after disposing of the body. As he straightens the tarp, she removes the bindings tying the still and already cooling body to the table sticky with blood. Waiting for him to finish, she gazes at the woman, who didn't even last a week. Crimson darkens her dark red hair further. That is correct.

One blue eye hangs from its socket. That's not the right shade of blue.

Grunting with her companion, the woman helps hoist the lacerated and broken body onto the tarp. "Time to dig another hole," he says with no emotion, rolling the body in the dark tarp and dragging it out.

Now alone, the woman grabs a mop, bucket, and rags. At least this room has adequate light. He wants to be sure he can see his victim. After multiple times refreshing the bucket, she is satisfied the room is clean enough to avoid punishment. Turning the light off, she exits with a sigh. It's time to look again.

CHAPTER ONE

Nightmare Ride

The blue cushioned seat adjusts to my shifting weight. Trees and sunny sky rush past my window as the train clanks along its winding track. Nature is beautiful, much more beautiful than the streets in my suburban childhood home. This is a new beginning.

I love my family deeply, but I can't take the constant worry and concern. At twenty-three, I have yet to live down the fact that I didn't go to college. Nothing in those schools ever appealed to me, so why should I subject myself to boring lectures and constant, unwanted party invites? When they aren't pushing me to make something out of myself, they are trying to set me up with men they met during whatever errand they were on. Romantic relationships have never been on my itinerary. I'm comfortable in my singleness, but I'm tired of being told I'm too pretty to be alone.

Don't get me started on their other concerns.

That's why I decided I need a change; a life where people don't know of my problems and feel the need to constantly bring them up. A place where people are not all over my life and spouting their concerns. I need peace outside of the life I had, a peace only the country can bring. I am ready for that peace.

My dry, sticky throat drags me from my thoughts of my mundane life. Standing, I stretch my cramped legs, keeping my moan low enough to not disturb the bald man sleeping in front of me. I walk in the direction of the dining car, looking for something to relieve my parched throat. One table holds a couple enjoying a snack together and smiling at each other like nothing else exists in this world. The rest of the car is empty, but the train doesn't have many passengers altogether. I ask for a bottle of water and head back to my poorly cushioned seat.

My phone pings as I sit, disrupting my intent to stare out my window some more. It's Ava.

Ava: Emma!!!

I sigh. Ava is like a sister to me, but she is a little overly excitable.

Me: Ava?

Ava: Are you there yet?

Me: No. I told you it's a four-hour ride. It's been two.

The bubbles pop up, telling me she's typing. They disappear, reappear, disappear, then reappear. I go back to contemplating the world passing by my window as she types and rethinks on repeat. My phone pings after a few minutes go by.

Ava: I know. I just can't believe you are doing this. Are you sure you want to pick up your entire life like this?

Me: I need a change. You know why I'm doing it.

Ava: Your family is only worried. I'm worried.

Me: I'm fine.

As my best friend types and retypes again, I take a swig of my icy water. I know what they're worried about. I wish they'd stop. As I said, I'm fine.

Ava: I just think you need to talk to someone, not run away.

Me: I'm sure you're aware I've talked to many someones. I'm not taking more sleeping pills. I spent half my life in a fog, Ava.

Ava: The nightmares have returned. Your parents told me. They say you're not sleeping again.

I groan, rolling my eyes at my parents' constant meddling. Why can't they leave this be?

Me: Well, no one needs to worry about me anymore.

Ava: Just because you're not here does not mean we aren't going to worry.

Snoring from the man in front of me drowns out my next groan.

Me: I don't want to talk about this anymore.

Ava: Fine, but I don't like that you left like this. You're going to be a servant. Who even uses newspapers to advertise jobs anyway, especially out of town?! And why on earth did they want you to mail your picture?

Me: It pays well. It's not there. Maybe they don't like technology. Also, they wanted to make sure I was the right fit for the job. I guess I needed to appear well put together.

Ava sends me the eye roll emoji but doesn't say anything else. The passing trees call me back to my window. I get her worry, but I need this. Ava sends another text.

Ava: I miss you.

Okay, she's got me there. I've spent my whole life playing and running around with Ava. She is the only thing that makes my decision hard.

Me: I miss you too. We can still visit each other.

Ava: Not the same.

My best friend follows her last text with every sad and crying emoji known to man. I smile, but it's not happy. I will definitely miss her. I hope we get to see each other often. My eyes grow heavy as I watch the scenery go by.

"Miss! Miss!"

With a scream, I fight off the hands shaking my shoulders. Get them off me!

"Miss!"

Heart beating wildly, I open my eyes, swatting at the bald man trying to restrain me. Not again! "Get off me! Don't hurt me, please! What do you want?!"

The bald man steps back in a hurry. "I'm sorry if I scared you, miss. You were screaming in your sleep."

His words hit me like a bucket of ice water, causing the world to make sense again. The heaviness of sleep releases my tortured mind as I pant like I've just run a marathon. I'm not back in that dark alley, bleeding from multiple cuts. There's no bloody knife lying next to me.

"I'm sorry," I whisper, voice trembling and unrecognizable.

Trying to cheer me up, the man smiles. "It's fine, miss. I'm just glad you're okay. Maybe this is Karma for me making you listen to my chainsaw running while I was asleep."

I muster a shaking smile and nod. "It's fine. You have nothing on my dad."

The bald man chuckles, turning to walk in the direction of the dining car. Glancing around, I see everyone is still looking at me. Some faces are full of sympathy and understanding. Other faces are just curious. A few look at me like I'm the most annoying person in the world for disturbing them.

This is what Ava was talking about. I woke her up with my screams during so many sleepovers. It's always the same. I'm putting the key in my door, exhausted and glad to be home. A man with a knife attacks from the darkness. He stabs me in the stomach, but I'm able to flee. I never make it far. He always tackles me in the alley beside my home, stabbing me over and over. There's always blood, so much blood.

Multiple therapists have tried to get to the bottom of my night terrors. None have been at all useful. They stick me on sleeping pills and stuff to drown out those nightmares but offer no other help. "It's only a dream," they always tell me.

It doesn't feel like a dream.

I can feel the eeriness surrounding me before the attack, making me try harder to hurry to get into the safety of my home as my key keeps missing its hole. My throat hurts with the scream that issues forth when I'm attacked, muffled by the gloved hand covering my mouth. The knife sends burning pain through my abdomen. The wound pulls as I flee, tearing open more. Asphalt scrapes my hands as I fall in the alley, smelling the stench of the dumpster beside us. I feel the knife enter over and over.

It feels so real.

Shoving all those terrible sensations behind the locked door in my mind only opened in sleep, I will my heart rate and breathing to calm, feeling my fingers begin to tingle. If I keep this up, I'm going to have a panic attack right here.

Breathe, Emma, breathe. It's just a dream. It can't hurt you.

By the time the train reaches my stop, I'm calm enough to stand, although my legs feel a bit like jello. Exiting the train, I grab my bags. I didn't bring much, just a suitcase on wheels and a little satchel. I want this to be a fresh start.

I grab a cab and have my bags in the trunk in no time. "Where to?"

Piercing blue eyes look at me from the rearview. "Restless Hills," I answer.

I can see my driver tense. "Are you sure?"

My eyes narrow in thought. "Yes. I have a job starting tonight. Is there a problem?"

"Not at all," he mumbles, switching the car into drive and pulling into traffic.

That's odd. If he doesn't relax his muscles soon, he's going to need some serious pain relievers. I try to lessen the tension. "Anything to do around here?"

My driver stays quiet for a few seconds. I'm about to repeat my question, but he finally says, "Not where you're going. Nothing good ever happens in Restless Hills. I'd suggest turning around and going home."

"Why?"

He sighs. "It's just... That town has a dark history. You should avoid it."

"It's called history," I counter, "because it's in the past. I'm sure I'll be fine."

"If you say so," he mutters so low I barely hear him.

Deciding to drop the subject, I ride in silence the rest of the way. The trees thin out, followed by rolling hills and fields of grass. After an hour of texting Ava, I notice my signal dropping off. "Are there no cell towers around here?"

Blue eyes look at me through the mirror again. "There are, but the hills make signal spotty at best. You won't get much where you're going."

I sigh. The cab comes to a stop at a turnoff, pulling off to the side of the road. "This is as far as I go," my driver tells me.

Confusion takes hold as I look around. "I don't see a town here."

The cabbie gets out and opens the trunk. I follow, still unsure what is going on. I look in every direction, seeing nothing but hills. "Why don't you take me the whole way?"

"Like I said," he explains, "nothing good ever happens in Restless Hills. I will stay out of it, and I warn you to do the same. I can take you back to the station for no extra charge."

I glare at him. "Why does everyone in my life try to tell me what to do? I know my mind."

My driver will not even look me in the eye. "The town is a mile that way," he points down the turnoff, "behind those hills there."

In a huff, I slap his cash into his hand, minus the tip I originally planned. Before I can even get my bags moving, he's turned around and heading back the way we came. Glad I wore sensible shoes, I start off in the direction he pointed. As I pass between those hills my driver pointed out, the fog starts to roll in. Visibility drops significantly very quickly.

I hope I don't get hit by a car.

CHAPTER TWO

Locked in the Past

The fog dissipates as quickly as it started, revealing a tiny little village surrounded by hills that are circled by hazy mist. The asphalt turns to dirt as the village comes into view. People walk the streets, quietly greeting one another. Others use keys to unlock shops, ready to receive customers. Not that it looks like there will be many customers.

The tiny village nestled within the rolling hills shows a row of houses circling the clutter of shops and market stalls. A large mansion sits at the back of the little town. No other roads enter or leave this dead-end town. I continue my walk in, watching people stop and stare at me. Clothes looking a little old-fashioned, townspeople stop what they are doing at the sight of me. The people look at me with a mixture of fear and hope, making me unsure of what they are expecting of me.

I hope this is not some kind of cult. A sense of dread builds within me at these stares. I watch some people jump as my eyes fall on them, and others actually fade into the shops lining the main street through town. My skin crawls with everyone's eyes following my every move. It is unnerving.

Besides the old-fashioned garments that seem to come from many eras, the town has other features that make it look like it is stuck in time. Roads are completely made of dirt. I don't see a single car anywhere. Is that a phone booth?

My contemplation of out-datedness is interrupted when my eyes meet a pair of golden-brown ones. These eyes aren't full of fear or hope, only burning curiosity. The man with dark hair and mesmerizing eyes is dressed in jeans and a dark red button-down shirt. He looks a bit more current than most of the others I have seen so far.

Something about this man tugs at me. Deep yearning bubbles up from within, confusing me. My heart skips a beat. Who is this man that is as captivated by me as I am of him? Why do I feel like I know him?

Breaking our staredown, the man with golden-brown eyes disappears into the building behind him. The spell lifts, making me blink. My world spins and tilts a little before settling down again. Who was that?

Taking a quick look at my phone, I realize I'm going to be late if I don't start moving. I notice I dropped the handle of my suitcase while staring at the curious man, so I pick it up and hurry toward the big house at the back of town with the wheels of my bag clattering over the rough dirt road. Once at its gates, I push the buzzer button on the wall. Curtains move, showing a pale face before covering their window again. I wait.

This house is massive. There are three stories, windows dotting the entire front of the mansion. The walls are a very dark blue, and the shutters are black. Wrapping around the house, the large porch is also painted black. It's dreary look-ing. A small shed or garage is off to the right. Dead-looking trees pepper the ground behind my new home. It's not winter, so I don't know why those trees look skeletal. You'd think they'd cut them down.

The heavy metal gates swing open with a loud screech.

As I walk up the sidewalk, I notice there is very little land-scaping. The lawn is trimmed perfectly, but no flowers or decorative bushes detract from the dreary landscape contained within these stone walls. A short woman with black hair swings the front door open as I climb the stairs. Dark eyes stare at me from a face that looks like it's stretched, thanks to the severity of her bun. She wears a black dress and apron.

She stares at me, not saying a word. "Emma Blackwood," I venture. "I'm here to—"

"Start employment," the woman finishes my sentence for me. Her voice is nasally, instantly setting me on guard.

"Yes, ma'am," I reply, getting the impression she expects formality. "You are?"

"Gertrude Cadwell," she says, turning around. "Follow me."

I follow her bouncing bun as it walks up the stairs in the center of the big central room. This guy must be loaded. Expensive dark blue and black carpets line the dark hard-wood floors, proceeding up the wooden staircase. Once on the second floor, we followed another blue running carpet down a side hall, leading to a door with another set of stairs.

It isn't until we're ascending these stairs that my guide speaks. "I am in charge of the house. You report directly to me and are to address me as madame. The only person above me is the master himself. You will assist with clean-ing, meal preparation, and running errands. Know that the master likes things proper and in their rightful places. Can you tie a tight bun?"

"Of course, madame," I say, smoothing my red locks.

"Good. He prefers his female staff to keep their hair impeccable and in a bun. Do you own any black dresses?"

I try to hold back a groan. I hate formality, but the pay will be worth it. "I'm sorry, madame. I do not."

She nods as if she expected the answer. "The previous women have left their dresses behind. Find one that fits as well as possible, and you will be fitted for new ones."

"What of the master of the house?" I'm getting nervous with all these rules. What is my new boss like?

"Master Radcliffe likes to keep to himself. You will only see him during meals," she informs me. "Do not speak to him unless he asks you a question, and never disturb him any other time."

We reach the third floor now. "This is the staff quarters. Any free time you have is to be spent here or in town, no wondering the house. Once you are settled, we will go over your duties, and I will show you the parts you are allowed to occupy."

Halfway down the black carpeted hall with dark-stained wooden walls and no decor, she opens a door to the left. "This is your room. There is a small kitchen at the end of the hallway by the stairs and a bathroom at the other."

"Do many people work here?"

She shakes her black bun. "Only you, the groundskeeper, and I. Master Radcliffe likes his privacy."

Following her into my accommodations, I feel my heart falter. There are no windows, the colors are just as dark as the rest of the house with black carpets and black sheets, and no decorations. A single lamp rests on the nightstand, and a dresser sits across from the foot of the bed.

"Can I add decor to my room?"

She nods. "You may personalize as you wish, but only in your room. Your room is expected to remain neat; no clothes on the floor, bed made, and no clutter."

As my eyes run over my tiny room again, I am startled to

see my black comforter looking back at me. A little squeak leaves my mouth, and my hand goes over my heart as I look at the golden eyes staring back at me.

"That's Angel," Gertrude explains. "She thinks this is her room."

Two pointed ears come into view as Angel's mouth opens wide in a yawn, sharp teeth glistening in the low light. A small purr issues forth as her eyes close. "She really blends in."

"Feel free to kick her out," my superior says in annoyance. "That pest always finds her way back in."

One golden eye opens, looking at the black-haired woman. In complete indifference, Angel snuggles in and goes back to sleep. "This was her home first," I say with a smile. "I don't mind sharing."

"As you wish. Take an hour to settle in. You will find dresses in the closet," she says, pointing to the door I failed to notice on the other side of the room.

"Thank y—"

She is already gone. I sit on the bed, causing the black cat to stir. Reaching out a welcoming finger, I let her sniff me before she rubs her cheek against my hand. I give her a good scratch. "Well, Angel, it looks like it's just you and me."

Purrs answer my words and scratches. Angel is small, probably the runt of the litter, but her fur is some of the softest I've ever felt. To show her pleasure, Angel's purrs increase in pitch. Much to Angel's unhappiness, I stand and put my suitcase on the bed.

I remove pictures of my family and line them on my dresser. The picture of Ava and I comes next. Ava is pushing me on the old wooden swing hanging from the giant oak tree in my front yard. Both of us are smiling with happiness.

I run my hand over the image of Ava's blond hair, missing her terribly.

Thinking of her, I open my phone. The signal is very weak, but maybe a text will go through. I tell her I made it, and I miss her. After putting my clothes in the drawers, I open the closet door. The closet is quite small; all the dresses organized neatly in rows by size. I find one that is a little loose in the chest area, but it fits better everywhere else. This will have to do.

The hair on my arm starts to stand on end. Angel's head shoots up, looking toward the empty corner of my room. Her ears go back, a growl vibrating in her chest. I stare at the corner, trying to discern what she sees.

There's nothing there. Goosebumps continue to work over the entirety of my tense body. Something feels wrong. It feels like I'm being watched. Angel unleashes a hiss at whatever has her undivided attention. When it looks like I may see a slight movement in that empty corner, I convince myself that my mind is playing tricks on me.

My hairs slowly relax as the feeling of being watched dissipates. Angel settles down, still staring at the corner and lashing her tail side to side. After what feels like an eternity, she lays her head on her paws, closing her big golden eyes. Whatever had her frazzled must be over now. A shiver runs up my spine.

CHAPTER THREE

Learning Duties

A knock sounds at my door, exactly one hour after I was told I'd have an hour. How did she time that so well? Did she show up early and wait until exactly one hour had passed?

Throwing one last glance at the creepy corner, I stand and open my door. "Follow me," Gertrude says, not even waiting for my response before she turns around and walks down the hall, dark bun bobbing with every step.

I follow her through the gloomy hall and down the stairs. Gertrude shows me various closets and empty guest rooms in this hallway. The room she spends the most time with involves an abundance of cleaning items. She explains each item and its use thoroughly. Who doesn't know how to use a broom?

After explaining, then quizzing me on the proper use of everything in the cleaning storage room, we head toward the main staircase. Gertrude stops at the top, pointing down the hall straight ahead.

"You are never to go there," she orders. "Those are Master Radcliffe's private rooms. Only those he truly trusts are allowed down that hallway."

I glance down the forbidden hall. The empty passage is even darker than the rest of the house. Staring down the emptiness in front of me sends chills down my spine. It feels as forbidden as she says it is. Turning back to my guide, I realize her tight bun is already bobbing down the staircase. I hurry to catch up. Once we reach the bottom, she turns to the right.

We enter a large white room. A huge wooden island sits in the center, scratches and cuts marring its worn surface. Aged black appliances sit along the wall, separated by more scarred countertops. Even with his obvious money, the owner of this mansion still has outdated appliances. What's with this town and its fear of the present?

"A cook visits three times a day," I'm informed. "He cooks, then leaves. You will help prepare each meal, serve it, then clean up after."

Without waiting for an answer, Gertrude walks through a side door. I follow, entering an enormous, beautiful dining room. The walls are constructed of the same dark wood I am finding usual in this giant house. Dark red and orange carpets cover the floor. The center of the room is dominated by a large wood table that looks like it can hold twenty people. Above the table is an elegant chandelier. An ancient grandfather clock sits on the opposite wall.

Gertrude goes over how I'm to serve him, then stands by the door to the kitchen to refill his drinks or get him anything he wishes. As we exit, we run into a blond man in dirty coveralls. Gertrude looks over the mess his boots have left, sending a glare at the man while he ignores her. "Isaac!"

I cringe at the anger in Gertrude's voice, but he blows her off. "Aren't you going to introduce me to my new co-worker, Gerty? That's kind of rude."

Red shades the ears under the tight, dark bun. "It's Gertrude!" She rolls her eyes at the tall man towering over her short stature. "Emma, this is Isaac, the groundskeeper."

I hold out my hand. "Pleased to meet you."

My hand falls when Isaac makes no move to take it.

Instead, he stares deep into my eyes without a single word. Fidgeting under his scrutiny, I'm unable to look anywhere but his face. I want to look away, but his eyes hold mine. My skin crawls under that intense gaze.

"Your eyes are a very interesting shade of blue, Emma," he finally breaks the disturbing silence. "They're the perfect mix of blue and green, like a clear ocean wave."

"Uh, thank you, sir," I mumble in discomfort.

"Anyway, Gerty," he says to my superior, increasing the heat in her eyes. "Where's the master of the house?"

"His study," she huffs.

Isaac heads toward the stairs without acknowledging her annoyed words. "That man. Do you know how to get mud out of carpets?"

"Not really, madame."

"Time to learn."

THE COOK TURNS out to be a very pleasant, portly man by the name of Peter. Peter has a knack for conversation, making me feel at ease for the first time since I arrived. He shows me the proper way to cut onions to avoid tears and how to arrange food on a plate so it looks as pleasing as it tastes. I'm arranging the food on the silver-plated serving cart when I hear the old clock chime five. Peter's demeanor changes in an instant, eyes shifting nervously.

"Better get out there, dear. He doesn't like waiting. I'll see you tomorrow," he says.

Peter removes his apron, rushing out the door. I push the cart through the entrance to the dining room, trying not to groan at the mess I have to clean up. The master of the house sits at the end of the table. A three-pronged candle stands in front of his plate, despite the bright light from above. It does nothing for lighting as it's weaker than what hangs above. A plate sits to his right. Gertrude didn't tell me why I have to set that place, since she said the clean plate will still require washing. A black coat and top hat hang on the coat rack by the door. A curved, wooden cane leans against the table. The bright light from above shines over everything.

The man sitting at the end has neatly trimmed salt and pepper hair, not a strand out of place despite his hat. His clean-shaven face remains downcast as I set the meal on the table, careful to do it exactly as Gertrude showed me. I pour him some ice water and squeeze the lemon into the glass before returning to wait by the door as instructed. It's time to wait for my orders.

Silence stretches through the long minutes, only broken by the sound of silverware on his plate. "Water," Master Radcliffe calls.

Not missing a step, I push the tray back to the far end of the table. Gertrude has informed me that the cart must be used each time to avoid messes. I refill his glass, squeezing a fresh lemon into the water. I'm careful to make sure to add just the right amount of juice to the clear liquid. My superior was very adamant that it must be perfect when instructing me.

As I pull away, my eyes meet his. I find myself lost in golden-brown eyes that remind me of the young man in the village. They have to be related, yet the difference is clear. Coldness radiates from these brown eyes, causing me to turn my head quickly. As I return to my spot, Gertrude sends me a glare from her supervisor's vantage point by the door leading to the dark hallway.

"Gertrude!"

I'm startled as he yells his head of staff's name, slamming his fist on the table and making the dinnerware jump above the wooden surface. His voice is raspy, as if it's either been used too much or not enough. The sound of it causes me to bite my lip. I'd rather hear nails on a chalkboard or a fork scraped across a plate. By his tone, I know he's not happy.

"Yes, master," comes the nasal reply.

"Where's my dessert?!"

Gertrude rushes over. Eyes widening, I examine the tray holding nothing but water and lemons. Did I forget dessert? I'm sure I grabbed everything. I'm screwing up my first day! This job is important for my new start, so I can't get fired.

"I'm sorry, master," Gertrude answers so fast she seems to be tripping over her own words. "I wasn't able to get to the bakery and hadn't realized we were out. I promise to have them tomor—"

Her voice falters as he turns his gaze on her. I can't see his face, but Gertrude turns white. I'm surprised to see her so flustered because the woman always seems unshakable. "Please. I promise to have them for you by lunchtime tomorrow."

"See that you do," he growls. "I won't be so forgiving tomorrow."

"Yes, master," Gertrude stammers, barely stopping herself from pulling at her perfect hair.

Master Radcliffe stands, using his cane to retrieve his coat and hat. Silence remains heavy in the air until the clicking of his cane disappears. Gertrude turns to me, fear warring with anger in her eyes. I'm not sure what I've done to deserve her fury, and I don't know why she looks so fearful. She seems to have earned steady employment.

"Finish your job and clean everything up," she snaps before running from the room.

I'm glad it wasn't my mistake. Gertrude's anger is enough to set me on edge, but his is scarier. The display only makes it clearer to me that I need to do my best not to cause any problems. I don't want his anger turned on me. Keeping my head down is a good idea.

IT TOOK FOREVER to clean up the dining room and kitchen. I'm now back in my dimly lit room, comfortable in my pajamas. The stiff fabric of the all-black dress is enough to make anyone uncomfortable. Releasing my hair from its bun feels like heaven. It's nice to be comfortable again after a long first day.

Checking my phone, I see my text to Ava still hasn't gone through. I try resending it, hoping to be able to talk to my friend. I curl my legs beneath me on my bed, and I'm overjoyed to see Angel circling me before cuddling up in my lap. On my way back to my room, I stopped at the very impressive library Gertrude had shown me. She said I could read any book as long as it found its way back.

Being tired, I grabbed the first book I found without registering what the cover even looked like. It seems to be a murder mystery. Opening the book, I run my hand over Angel as I read, her soft purrs vibrating in my lap. This is the perfect end to a stressful day. The purrs melt my tension away. I lose myself in the world written in these pages, relaxing in an alternate reality.

Angel tenses before I even finish the first chapter. Lowering the book, I see her slowly stand, tail thrashing to and fro. Her nose is pointed at the same empty corner again. Growls echo in the quiet room. She takes a few steps toward the corner. Goosebumps litter my flesh as the feeling of being watched returns. I slowly close my book, not taking my eyes from the empty corner. It thumps to the floor as I try to place it on the nightstand without looking.

A sense of doom courses through me when I slowly uncurl my legs and stand. As I inch toward the door, the feeling of dread increases. Angel walks to the edge of the bed, hissing as her head circles like she's following movement. I realize she's watching something coming my way. My heart freezes in my chest.

I inch back against the wall by the bed, trying to keep the distance between me and whatever spooked my furry companion. Nothing is visible, but the black cat's reaction is all I need to know something is wrong. My muscles ache with tension as Angel's eyes reach me. I feel a warm breath hit my face.

CHAPTER FOUR

Flaky Sweetness

D abbing a little concealer over the bags under my eyes, I examine my reflection. I believe it's safe to say that I didn't sleep well last night, at all. The feeling of an additional presence disappeared after that breath in my face, but I couldn't calm my racing heart enough to sleep. Something was there, and it felt menacing. It took everything I had not to make a run for the front door. I was ready to walk home if I had to.

I take a deep breath. Shivers still run through me. My need for flight has disappeared. There has to be another explanation. Angel's action spooked me and made me imagine things. That's the only logical explanation. I need a reasonable explanation after a night like that. Logic doesn't help me sleep. I wish I can be like Angel and just doze as soon as the presence vanishes.

Sighing, I give up on wishes that have no chance of fulfillment and pull my hair up. After my bun is secured, I inspect it carefully. It should pass. I don't see any loose strands, and making it tighter would end in me being bald. Feeling like I can't do any better than I have, I step away from the bathroom mirror. My phone pings.

Ava: OMG!!! Emma! I was so worried!!!! Why did you wait til now to tell me you made it?!

I guess my text finally went through. Examining my phone, I see a spotty, but improved signal. The time shows I

have a couple of minutes before Gertrude comes in search
of me for a good scolding. I need to communicate with my
friend.

*Me: Ava. The signal is terrible here. I've been trying to send
that since yesterday.*

Ava: I'm so glad you're okay. What are you up to?

Not wanting to push my luck, I begin walking as I type. I
can see Gertrude being the kind of supervisor that expects
her underlings to be early. After witnessing her humiliation
at supper yesterday, I don't think she'll be very forgiving of
me this morning. It's better to be on the safe side.

*Me: My duties are just starting. I'll scrounge some change
together. I promise I will call you from the phone booth on my
first free day. I'll keep trying to text you every day.*

Ava: A phone booth!!!

My signal drops completely. By the time I'm on the
ground floor, I can tell it's not coming back. I flip the volume
to silent and get to my duties. Peter is in the kitchen as I
enter, whipping up some kind of fancy omelet. After seeing
the meal he prepared last night, I would love to try his
cooking.

He smiles when he sees me. "Sorry for the rude exit,
dear. Master Radcliffe doesn't like people in the house past
their appointed time."

I accept his apology and work on getting the cart set up.
The sound of plates and the water container hitting the
metal cart echo in the closed room. Delicious scents fill the
kitchen, making my mouth water. After Peter departs, I
groan at the mess left behind. How can one omelet make
such a mess?

I enter the empty dining room. Both Gertrude and the
master of the house are absent. Unsure what to do, I stand at
my station. Time ticks by as my mind begins to wander.

There's still no one here after fifteen minutes. How long should I stand here? I'm sure I'll get in trouble if I move.

Gertrude enters after I've been standing at my post for over twenty minutes. "The master will not be attending breakfast this morning."

Great. Thanks for telling me. My eyes move down to the plate, contemplating if I'm allowed to taste the wasted food. My thoughts must be plain on my face. Gertrude glares at me. "Throw that out. It is meant for Master Radcliffe only, and he doesn't like reheated food. See me in the library after you've cleaned up."

With that, she turns and walks away, leaving me to clean up that massive mess from an uneaten breakfast. Wasting food has always made me uncomfortable, but I don't want to get fired over eggs, no matter how delicious they look and smell. My heart aches as the perfectly folded omelet slips into the trash. Stuck on food is stubborn. It takes more time than I'd like to finish the dishes.

GERTRUDE IS MOVING the broom back and forth over the uncarpeted areas of the expansive library when I enter. The light of the fireplace glows over the shelves built into the walls, warming the room and empty blue armchair in front of it. More books than I can count fill the shelves. It's a dream come true to live somewhere with a library this size. I used to spend entire days in the local library at home.

"Madame?"

Barely acknowledging my presence, the black-haired woman finishes her task before addressing me. She hands me a piece of paper and a square of thick card stock. "This note authorizes the purchase of three servant's dresses for you. The other is a card that authorizes you to use the Master's credit *only for official business.*"

What does she think? I'm going to go on a shopping spree? "Where do I find the seamstress?"

Gertrude grabs her duster and goes back to work. "Ask a local. It's not my problem. Stop at the bakery and get a dozen of the Master's favorites. They'll know what you mean. Remember, you are still on the clock, so don't take your time."

The urge to roll my eyes is hard to resist, but I somehow manage to keep my annoyance to myself. I run upstairs to grab my purse. I hope one of the townspeople will talk to me. Gertrude's lack of help is frustrating. The population of this little town seemed almost frightened of me when I first entered their home, but I don't think I have time to wander around looking for the shop. I don't want to deal with Gertrude being angry because I'm late.

As soon as I enter my room, Angel stretches and yawns, then asks for a scratch. After obliging her, I grab my purse from the nightstand and head out. Right before I reach the stairs down to the second floor, I freeze. The familiar prickly feeling of being watched tingles all over. Hair on my arm begins to stand on end as the goosebumps I'm becoming acquainted with pepper my skin. The floor creaks behind me.

My breath catches in my throat, and I turn. I observe the dark, gloomy hallway that looks to be empty. My heart races as the feeling of dread increases. Heart thumping against my breast bone so hard it hurts, I scan the area. Movement pulls my attention to the center of the hall a few doors down. I stare intently, waiting to see it again. When nothing happens, I take a cautious step backward, hand reaching for the doorknob.

That's when I finally see it. There's an indent in the spotless black carpet, creating further shadow in the darkness. The impression looks like that of a shoe like someone is standing in that spot. As if the invisible entity realizes its error, the floor creaks as the imprint eases and disappears. No more footsteps show on the carpet, but I'm not waiting around to see it happen again.

Without further thought, I turn the knob and dash down the stairs, breath coming from my lungs in harsh gasps. My heart continues to try to break free from my chest. As I exit onto the second floor, I slow my pace but keep my steps brisk. I can only imagine if Gertrude caught me running.

SURPRISINGLY, I am able to get directions for the seamstress. The little shop is not far down the main stretch, and I find it with ease. I'm standing in a much too big dress with pins stuck everywhere. Light brown hair circles around me as the seamstress does her work, measuring tape looped around the back of her neck. Her fingers are quick and agile.

When done, she tells me to stop tomorrow. Master Radcliffe gets expedited service, by the looks of it. For some reason, that doesn't surprise me. Maybe it's the fact his house sits over the town like a lord's castle. Asking for the direction of the baker, I leave in pursuit of my next errand.

The baker turns out to be a stout, gray-haired woman with flour on her nose. I give her the order, and she knows exactly what I'm after. "So, you're the new help?"

I nod. "Just started yesterday."

This old woman seems very kind and warm. I feel comfortable around her. She feels like the grandmother I always imagined. Mine died before I was born, but I always pretended to visit them like my friends always got to. She fits my childhood imagination perfectly.

"Best of luck to you," she says, pulling a white box from the shelf beneath fresh cupcakes.

I watch as she places some kind of crumbling pastries covered in chocolate into the white box. I've never seen them before. Her warm chuckles sound at my open curiosity. "I call them Amelia's Tears, after my inspiration."

I do see the resemblance to teardrops. "That's kind of a sad name."

The old woman smiles, but the warmth is gone. "It's a sad story. Here. Try one, on the house."

She hands me a chocolate-covered teardrop. Taking a bite of the pastry, I can't stop the moan as the flaky dessert with just the right amount of doughiness hits my tongue. The gooey chocolate explodes, filling my mouth with the perfect level of sweetness. It's even still warm. This is heaven in a dessert.

"Delicious, isn't it?"

Startled by the deep voice behind me, I start coughing as flakes enter my throat without permission. The baker hands me a glass of water, trying to help me wash the pastry down my throat. I gulp the cool liquid down and try not to choke more. My throat feels raw. Still coughing, I turn to my source of startlement.

"I didn't mean to kill you," the man laughs, amusement dancing in his golden-brown eyes.

Shock hits me for the second time in less than a minute when I realize it's the dark-haired man I saw when I entered through the fog. He's staring at me, a smile brightening up his handsome face and making me feel breathless. "I'm sorry," I say.

"No need to apologize," he counters with a very addictive chuckle. "I scared you."

I hold my hand out. "I'm Emma."

He takes my hand in his strong, yet soft, fingers, bringing it to his lips. "It's a pleasure to meet you, Emma. I'm Edgar."

My heart skips a beat as his lips brush my knuckles. Edgar's eyes suck me into their depths. I feel lost but found at the same time. I slowly remember to breathe. It's hard. He takes my breath away.

Grabbing my white box of mouth–watering pastries, he offers me his arm. I take it without thought. Something about my arm in his feels like it's meant to be. I try to make conversation. "You like these pastries?"

We exit the bakery before he answers. "They're my absolute favorite. Only Mrs. Jones knows how to make them. They're a bit of a delicacy in this small town. So, you work at the Radcliffe Manor?"

With my affirmative answer, he starts leading me in the direction of my new, spooky home. "How did you know?"

Edgar's laugh makes me feel warm in all the right places. "Only that old fart would make anyone wear a bun that tight."

Laughs burst from me. "They are a bit uncomfortable."

"I bet," he chuckles.

We talk for a bit, getting to know each other as we pass curious faces along the street made of only dirt. I can't help but wonder how he is connected to my employer. Their eyes show a connection that can only be made by DNA. Their faces also have a similar shape.

Reality hits me as I realize he's talking about how old the

manor is. I can't help but ask, "Has anyone ever mentioned anything strange happening in the house?"

"Strange how?" he asks, eyes betraying curiosity.

"I don't know," I say, nervous all of a sudden. "Unexplainable and creepy?"

The amusement returns to his beautiful eyes. "Are you asking if it's haunted?"

Feeling unsure, I only nod. He smiles. "Not any more than anywhere else in Restless Hills."

Once we reach the impenetrable metal gate, I turn to thank him. My hand returns to his lips, but he freezes, lips still on my knuckles. I have felt nothing but warmth from this gentleman, but anger and hatred turn his eyes cold as he looks behind me. It scares me. The look in his eyes brings fear.

Turning to follow his gaze, I see Master Radcliffe walking toward the front door. Isaac watches the exchange with curiosity from the corner of the dark blue house. Master Radcliffe returns Edgar's stare with equal coldness, only his is indifferent whereas Edgar's is angry. Master Radcliffe sends Edgar a smirk before entering the house.

"What was that?" I whisper.

Edgar snaps out of his glare directed at the door the master walked through. "Nothing, dear Emma. I hope to see you around."

Edgar turns and walks back to town, throwing me one last wave and smile. This is curious.

CHAPTER FIVE

Moving Ashtrays

The vacuum drowns out all thoughts as it rolls over the dark red carpet. Shifting the black armchair in front of yet another fireplace covered with a few candles and small game trophies, I vacuum the spot underneath. The two black couches prove a little harder to move, but I manage. I'm getting a workout at this job. I never expected cleaning to be this hard.

Pulling out the attachment, I vacuum the cigar ashes under the table holding an antique radio, green-shaded lamp, and ceramic ashtray. Once the carpet is spotless, I roll the vacuum to the door and grab the feather duster, wondering if I should have done this first. It won't matter. There's very little dust, thanks to Gertrude's diligence. Before I can turn around, I'm startled by a loud thump.

I turn quickly, seeing the ashtray laying on the floor face up. That's odd. I must've bumped the table when I was vacuuming under it and not noticed the tray move to the edge. After dusting the table, I place the dark green tray back in front of the lamp and make sure there's no way it can fall off again. I move on to the tables by the couches.

After removing the almost non-existent dust on the frequently cleaned furniture, the thud makes me turn again. Chills run through me as I see the ashtray is now on the floor, on the opposite side of the chair. I know I was careful to put it where it couldn't fall. Even if I hadn't, there is no way it could've landed on that side of the chair. How did it get there?!

I place it back on the table, spinning when I hear another sound behind me. A stuffed squirrel lies on the freshly vacuumed carpet instead of its place on the mantle. My heart races as I look for the source of the disturbance. Nothing but the squirrel is out of place. My heart begins to quicken.

Fear causes me to finish my task as fast as possible, returning the ceramic tray, dead animals, and candles to their rightful places countless times. I rush out, heart bouncing in my chest, before it can happen again. Edgar seemed to think I had nothing to fear, but I doubt his words. I'm starting to wonder if this job is truly worth the pay.

ONCE AGAIN, I'm standing by the serving cart, silently waiting for Master Radcliffe to need anything. Peter didn't seem flustered that his omelet wasn't eaten. He said he's used to it by now. Such a waste of delicious food is disappointing. These delicacies deserve to be eaten.

"Water!"

I rush over with my cart to fill his glass and add a squeeze of lemon, careful to not make eye contact this time to avoid Gertrude's glare. My cheek feels like it's on fire from his intense golden-brown gaze I try to ignore. I try to hide my unease and act professional. Gertrude isn't one to let anything slip. When the lemon is devoid of any more juice, I walk back to my post.

My mind wanders, but I keep my ears open. Those eyes. There's something about those golden-brown eyes. In

Edgar, they hold a warmth that draws me in and is captivating. Master Radcliffe has a coldness in his gaze that is frightening. How can two men wear the same eyes so differently?

Speaking of frightening. I can't seem to get my mind off the strange happenings in this creepy, old mansion. Something is not right. Or am I imagining it all? Are my dreams leaking into my conscious hours? The thought sends chills through me.

"Ahhh," my employer's pleased sigh reaches my ears. "You kept your promise, Gertrude."

"Of course, Master Radcliffe," her nasal voice says, sounding relieved.

Sure, take the credit.

I've never seen a pastry enjoyed as delicately as the master of Radcliffe Manor enjoys the chocolaty goodness in his hands. My mouth waters at the thought of that delicious dessert and the man I met in pursuit of it. After every single crumb is devoured, Master Radcliffe pushes himself up with his cane before clicking toward the coat rack. Gertrude hurries to help him into his coat, and he places the top hat on his head.

I listen to the click of his cane recede down the dark hall. Gertrude turns to me. "Did you finish the den?"

"Yes, madame," I reply, trying to suppress the shudders that threaten to overtake me.

"Good." The black bun bobs with her nod. "Clean up here, then you're free for the rest of the night."

She says that like it's easy to clean up the mess Peter leaves in his haste to depart. I've never seen someone get food in so many places while cooking. Mom used to say that messes are a sign of a good cook. I'm not so sure, but it seems true when it comes to Peter. At least, I'm assuming it tastes as good as it looks. If only I could try some.

AFTER SPENDING an hour bent over the kitchen sink scrubbing pots, the heat and steam of the shower feel like a dream come true. I sigh as the warmth melts my sore muscles. It's times like these that I don't mind the emptiness of the servant's quarters. There's no competition for bathroom time, and I can shower as long as I want. No one can complain about my relaxing use of the hot water.

Once my skin is a desired shade of red, I work on cleaning myself, looking forward to my book and snuggles with Angel. Thinking of that strange presence, I slow my movements. I hope it leaves me alone tonight. I can use a little sleep. Although, just the thought of everything going on may only increase my nightmares.

Turning the water off, I pull back the curtain and scream at the horror standing beside the tub. A woman with red hair stands right outside the curtain. She stares at me with eyes clouded over. I begin to tremble as I take her in.

She stands naked, blood running down her ravaged body and onto the sand-colored tiles. As it continues to run onto the floor, the thick crimson puddle spreads. Her dark red hair is matted with a darker crimson, hard and sticky. A few fingers are missing from one mangled hand. The other hand hangs limply, arm broken in multiple places. Lacerations cover her entire naked body. Pale skin is absent from spots on her legs, abdomen, and chest. The most horrifying part is the huge gash in her throat.

She points at me with her missing finger, cloudy eyes trying to convey something I can't quite place. Blood pours from the mangled stump of what used to be her index finger, splashing to the floor like a waterfall hitting rocks below. More blood spills from her lips as she opens her mouth. It runs down her body in rivers, leaving a dark stain in its wake.

There is so much thick, crimson blood. Bile threatens to surface, strengthened by the numbing fear that freezes my entire body. I can't breathe. I can't run. I have nowhere to run anyway. She's standing between me and the door. I don't dare try to go around her.

The dead woman tries to speak. Warmth hits my face as her action causes blood to spray from the ruin of her throat, peppering me and the surrounding surfaces. More blood runs from the cut and down over her tormented body like a river that has broken free of its dam. This time, the blood doesn't stop flowing to reveal a stain. It continues, covering the once clean floor beneath her feet. Not a single tile remains untouched by the torrent.

I can no longer scream. Sound will not exit no matter how hard I try. It's like my insides are frozen with fear. Looking down, I see the woman's blood covering my freshly cleaned skin. I can feel drops running down my face. It only smears when I try to wipe it away and is now on my palms as well.

The tortured woman tries to speak again, spraying more sticky liquid. This time, my screams succeed as I try to melt into the wall behind me. My feet slip on the slick ceramic surface of the tub. Pain seers through my lower back when I land, causing me to squeeze my eyes shut. Afraid of what I'm about to see, I open my eyes.

She's gone. Her mangled body and blood are nowhere to be seen. Looking down, I notice I no longer see the blood on my freckled skin. I can still feel it. The sticky feeling will not abate, and it continues to make me gag. Turning the water on hotter than I can stand, I speed scrub the invisible red stains off me, watching the area outside the ceramic tub. I'm not sure how I did it, but I manage to scrub the non-existent blood from my now sore skin. I towel off, trying to convince myself I'm seeing things as I get dressed. My dreams have turned into nightmares.

As I turn to leave, something catches my eyes. There's a bloody handprint on the doorknob.

CHAPTER SIX

Pudgy Black Hen

The sky brightens into shades of pink and orange as I sit on the wooden steps leading to the porch around the house. I had promised myself that I would try to get some sleep once my heart stopped hammering, and I could catch my breath, but it never happened. I've spent the whole night sitting on this dark porch, trying to convince myself I was seeing things in the bathroom last night.

It's a good thing I'm used to not getting much sleep. That couldn't have been real. I've been sitting here, shivering in the chill of the night air, trying to tell myself it wasn't real. All the blood was gone. There's no way that much blood would just disappear. The handprint, I can't explain, but there's a logical explanation for it. Ghosts aren't real.

It sure felt real.

Bringing my hands to my face, I rest my elbows on my knees, rubbing my eyes and groaning. I want to scream, but I don't want to wake the master of the house. I sit up and scratch at my skin. That blood felt real as it dripped down my face and body. The warm tickle as it ran down my face will add new horror to my nightly terrors. I shudder, holding back the bile threatening to exit at the memory.

My fidgeting is interrupted by the sound of the front door opening. When I see Gertrude, I jump to my feet. "Madame?"

Even this early, her clothes and black bun are pure perfection. "What are you doing out here at this hour?"

"I couldn't sleep and thought the fresh air would help."

There's no way I'm telling her what I saw. Crazy isn't something that will look good on my resume. She doesn't need to know I'm seeing dead people and feeling their blood on my skin. The fact that I can't sleep because I'm convinced this place is haunted doesn't need to be made known. Gertrude would only laugh and send me packing.

She stares at me a bit, eyes looking thoughtful. Can she tell I'm not being a hundred percent truthful? I didn't actually lie to her, just omitted. Does that make my actions any more excusable? I don't have to lie to not be truthful. If I would have to guess, Gertrude wouldn't take well to knowing her staff is hiding things.

I open my mouth to try to sound more convincing but am interrupted by the sounds of booted feet stomping up the steps. Isaac stops beside me, coveralls as dirty as the last time I saw him. This is only our second meeting, but I'm already wondering if he is ever clean. After our last meeting, it wouldn't surprise me to learn that he's remaining filthy just to aggravate Gertrude.

As if proving my point, Gertrude takes in his muddy boots, placing her hands on her hips. "Where do you think you are going with those muddy boots?"

"I have business with the master of the house, Gerty," he says, taking another step.

Hands still on her hips, Gertrude blocks his path with an impressive glare and leans forward. "I'm tired of cleaning up your mess."

"It's your job, isn't it?" Before Gertrude can reply, he continues, "You know, Gerty? You shouldn't stand too long like that. Someone might see and think you're a pudgy black hen and look for eggs."

Do not laugh, Emma. Do not laugh. It hurts not to laugh.

While Gertrude recovers, the blond groundskeeper slips past her and into the house. I look down as she turns her glare toward me. "You are to pick up your dresses today?"

I clear my throat a few times to buy a little space to hide my mirth. "Yes, madame."

She huffs. "Take a free day, then. Your only duty is to pick up your dresses."

I nod in relief, glad I can get out of the house for a little. My supervisor watches, as if waiting for me to give her a reason to release her fragile temper. A few seconds later, she gives up and turns toward the door. As Gertrude opens the door to return to her duties, Angel comes running out, hissing and swiping her claws at the flustered black-haired woman. The cat's fur stands straight up to make herself look bigger.

"Stupid pest!" Angel doesn't even acknowledge Gertrude's insult, disappearing around the house in a black blur. "Wretched beast. I hope you don't come back someday!"

I'd rather have the cat here than you.

Gertrude stomps into the house, oblivious to my inner thoughts. I take a minute to compose myself and give her a few moments to disappear. When I enter, her black bun is nowhere in sight. At least I won't have to pull my hair into that nasty bun today. My scalp will thank me.

Once in my room, I slip into a little blue sundress and head in the direction of the bathroom. I hesitate before placing a cautious foot on the cool tile. Glancing around, I inspect every corner before moving to the vanity above the sink. Keeping an eye on the area covered by the mirror, I quickly add just a little make-up. I survey myself in the reflection, hoping I look as nice as I feel.

I try to tell myself I'm not trying to catch the attention of a handsome young man with lovely golden-brown eyes. Deep down, I know that's a lie. There's something about him, something I can't quite place. Whatever it is, I'm pulled to it. Besides, a little pleasant company wouldn't hurt my free day at all.

I'm thankful my bathroom experience is uneventful. Stopping in my cramped room, I slip on a pair of sandals and grab my purse. Once outside again, I breathe a sigh of relief. Nothing strange has happened on my way out. Maybe my mind feels it has scared me enough for now. I'm not sure how much more of my twisted imagination I can take.

I regret that thought as I begin the short walk into town. Something sounds off with my footsteps. I stop but hear nothing. I'm sure my feet aren't that loud. After a few more steps, I change my pace. That's when it hits me. There's someone following me.

Spinning, I look for whoever is behind me, my heart rate rapidly increasing. "Who's there?"

Silence is my only answer as I stand alone on the dirt road. The feeling of being watched returns. I turn with a spin of my red hair, walking at a brisk pace with the following footsteps right behind. My foot hits a rock, causing me to trip. The footsteps stop.

Standing, I turn. A faint footprint stares back at me from the dirt right beside my feet, much too large to be my own. Panicked, I break into a run, covering the remaining distance to town as fast as possible. I no longer hear the footsteps, but I don't want to wait around for them to return.

As my feet reach the cement sidewalk, I spin. Nothing is out of place behind me. While I catch my breath and wait for my heart to slow, I dust the dirt from my earlier stumble off my blue dress. Sweat beads my forehead, so I dab it away. When I feel composed, I move about my day.

My first stop is the phone booth. I can't wait to hear Ava's voice. I need something solid to ground me. I feel like control is slipping. Rummaging in my purse, I find a small handful of change. I pull out my cell phone, look up Ava's number, deposit the change into the phone, then dial my best friend.

It rings three times. "Hello?"

My heart lifts at the sound of my best friend's voice. "Ava!"

"Oh my God, Emma!" I pull the receiver off my ear as she squeals in delight after I feel my brain vibrate. "I never answer calls if I don't know the number, but I know you said you'd call from a phone booth."

She's no longer squealing, but her high-pitched excitement still hurts. "I got a free day today. How are things?"

"It's about time," she exclaims. "The usual here. Your parents are very worried." At my groan she hurries on, "I'm not trying to guilt-trip you, Emz. I'm just letting you know."

"Ava, I don't really want to get into this. We only have as long as it takes for my change to run out, and I don't have much," I plead. "How's Jared?"

Operation change subject is a success as Ava begins to gush over her latest man. After a little while, I cut in. "You've been together for six months now?"

I can hear her smile in her voice. "I know, right? I know I have sampled the goods a bit, but he feels like the one. He's not like all those other douchebags I've dated."

I roll my eyes thinking of her past interests. "You can say that again. You were never good at picking them."

"Hey," she giggles. "Don't make me reach through this phone and smack you."

I laugh. "I guess there's one advantage to a long-distance friendship."

"I may not have the best track record, but at least I have a record."

"Yeah," I laugh again, "I don't really want a record with anyone from our little suburb."

We talk like this until my change gives out. Once I get a minute warning, we say our goodbyes. I do not tell her of the creepy things happening. My best friend will only worry. I don't want her to worry more than she already does.

"What's with the huge smile?"

At the sound of his deep voice after I exit the booth, my heart climbs into my throat, and I let out a yelp. If it wasn't for my impending heart attack, I'd smile at his laughter. So far, our meetings haven't started in a pleasant way. He startles me every single time, which is twice.

"Didn't mean to scare you again," he chuckles.

I smile. "You seem to be making it a habit."

Edgar's eyes twinkle at my teasing. "How about I buy you lunch to make it up to you?"

The gorgeous man wraps my arm in his and leads me down the sidewalk. People we walk past pause and sidestep from our path. I still see fear in their eyes, but they're starting to shine with something else when they see me walking through their town with one of their own leading me. I can't place it. It looks a little like hope. That doesn't make any sense.

Peter owns this little diner, but he's at the manor preparing lunch for Master Radcliffe right now. Edgar seems fond of the cook, saying how his food is the best. I haven't had a chance to try his cooking, but I'm sure it's as delicious as it looks and smells. Even if Peter isn't in the kitchen of the diner now, I look forward to a little taste of what it might be like.

Hot, creamy cheese fills my mouth as I bite into my mouth-watering grilled cheese sandwich I had just saturated with creamy tomato soup. Edgar grins around the burger currently stuffed in his mouth, brown eyes dancing with amusement. This town seems less dark in his presence. He shines like a beacon to me, guiding me out of the dark and into the light.

Edgar shakes his head, still smiling. I'm intrigued. "What?"

He laughs. "I take you out to eat in a diner full of delicious home-cooked food, tell you to get whatever you like, and you choose grilled cheese."

"What? Grilled cheese is the best comfort food," I say around my next bite with no shame.

I'm getting really used to this guy's laugh. "I can't argue with that. So, who were you before coming to the little town of Restless Hills?"

I sigh. "Just a girl looking to get away from smothering family and friends. My life isn't that interesting."

Curiosity is clear in his gaze, but he senses I don't want to talk about any of it and doesn't ask. "I'm sure you're very interesting."

It's my turn to laugh. "Nope. I'm pretty normal."

"I look forward to learning what you think is normal."

I blush at his words. Lunch continues like this; lots of questions and compliments from both sides. As we leave, the employees and fellow diners flash Edgar bright smiles and goodbyes. Edgar returns their warmth with his own and leads me out. He seems to be very popular in this tiny village.

I'm lost in his smile and conversation as we walk. The bell on a door jingles before I realize we are entering a building. Sweet goodness fills my senses. I look over to see the little old lady with the flour on her nose. The thought of one of those pastries melting in my mouth makes it water prematurely.

The baker's face lights up when she sees who enters. "Young Edgar! The usual?"

"Please, Mrs. Jones, but make it two today," he answers. "How's the husband?"

Mrs. Jones's smile widens further at the sight of me, that same unknown look twinkling in her eyes. "Moody as always, Edgar. How are you enjoying the town, miss?"

"It's unique," I say.

They both chuckle. The gray-haired woman hands Edgar two Amelia's Tears. He leads me to a small white table, and we sit. Ever the gentleman, Edgar pulls out my chair for me. I've never been treated like this before. It leaves me both uncomfortable and overjoyed at the attention. Dating was never a thing for me, as it was for Ava.

"You shouldn't keep spending money on me," I reason as my mouth sinks into the heavenly pastry.

"You need a proper welcome, dear Emma," he counters. "I won't go broke treating you for a day."

He bursts out laughing. "What?" I ask.

"You got a little something..." He touches the corner of his lip.

Embarrassed, I quickly wipe my mouth. "Did I get it?"

Edgar only laughs harder. "No. You just smeared it. Let me..."

Before either of us realizes what's happening, his thumb is on my lower lip, wiping across it. His captivating eyes widen as I sit frozen. We stare into each other's eyes for what feels like an eternity. Jumping back, he apologizes while wiping chocolate off his thumb.

My voice finally finds me. "It's okay."

"No," he shakes his head, "it's not. That was awfully forward of me. I'm sorry. I didn't realize what I was doing until it was too late."

My hands covering his larger ones halt his rambling. "I said it is fine, and I mean it."

My actions finally stop his worry, and we enjoy the rest of the pastries. Edgar shows me around town, introducing me to its residents. After treating me to supper, despite my objections, he walks me back to the manor while carrying the dress bags over his shoulders. With all he's done for me today, I tried to insist I carry my own dresses. He declined and told me a gentleman wouldn't allow that.

"The town's people seem to like you," I mention.

Edgar chuckles. "I'm seen as the town golden boy."

"So, I attracted a good one?" Edgar's hand squeezes mine. My curiosity gets the better of me. "They seem touchy about Master Radcliffe like they fear him."

"Master Radcliffe," Edgar says with a grimace as if he just ate something sour, "basically runs this town. He does it by bullying and fear."

My smile falls hearing this about my employer. I know he isn't looked well upon, but I'm still surprised at the animosity. "Are you two somehow related?" At the loss of warmth in his stunning eyes, I hurry on. "I'm just curious. You both have the same eyes and similar faces. I just thought you might be."

"In a way," he says in a manner that cuts off further questions.

We walk in silence the rest of the way. As we near the dark house, all the fear and uncertainty Edgar has made me forget comes back. I'm so worried about what this night might come with. I turn to the stiff man beside me. "I'm sorry. I didn't mean to pry."

Looking down at my feet, I watch the dirt move as I push it with the tip of my sandal. I hear his sigh. His thumb and finger embrace my chin, pulling my face up to meet his eyes. "It's fine. Just a touchy subject."

A meow interrupts my next thought. Angel is weaving around Edgar's feet. He bends down, running his hand over her soft fur. "Hey there, Angel."

"You know Angel?"

Edgar stands. "Yeah. She tends to wander around town. She hasn't been around much for a couple of days."

Those golden-brown eyes twinkle as he finishes that last sentence. Before I can ask him anything else, he brings my hand to his lips and hands me my dresses. "I hope to see you more soon."

I watch his retreating back as he heads back toward town. Angel lets out a soft meow like she misses him already. "Me too, Angel. Me too."

Dread builds in me as I follow the black cat up the stairs on the dark porch.

CHAPTER SEVEN

Living Nightmare

I walk up the stone steps to my welcoming abode. Darkness surrounds me, stars shining bright overhead. The moon is full, illuminating the light beige siding and blue door. Opening my pink cloth handbag, I fumble for my keys.

Their jingle echoes in the quiet air as I take the metal ring of keys from my light pink bag, the plastic sleeping cat holding them in one place. Out of nowhere, an unease settles over me, a feeling of being watched that causes my skin to crawl. A meow pulls my attention to the black cat sitting in my window.

I breathe deep, hoping she's the one I feel watching me. Something tells me I'm wrong. My hands shake, causing the key to miss its hole and barring me from the safety that is my home. The metal sound of the key scraping over the lock makes me cringe.

I turn at the sound of footprints. Gasping, I recognize the man in front of me, even though I can't quite make out his face in the shadows. A gloved hand covers my mouth as I let out a scream that is strong enough to hurt my lungs.

Metal shines in the light of the full moon, then pain sears and spreads through my abdomen. Somehow, I break free, running for the alley beside my house. Blood runs down my skin, soaking into my expensive dress, a dress I treasure as a gift from someone I care strongly for. The smell of the dumpster in this alley assaults my nostrils, but I don't care.

Before I make it far, I'm tackled, hands scraping the ground below my body. Rolling over, I plead for my life. My attacker does

not listen, plunging the knife into me over and over. The last
things I notice as darkness takes me are the smell of rotting trash
and someone screaming my name.

Screaming, I jump into a sitting position, clutching the
nightgown over my rapidly beating heart. After a few
seconds of fighting my restraints, I realize the hands holding
me down are only my heavy blankets. I free the arms
captured by my black comforter. Quickly, I lean over to turn
on the dull light on my nightstand.

I try hard to calm my frantic nerves, recognizing my
small, dark room. Angel sits on my dresser, reminding me of
the cat that showed up in my dream for the first time. My
dream has always been the same. How did she make an
appearance this time? Why did it change?

Nothing in that dreaded nightmare has ever changed in
the past. Why now?

Taking deep breaths, I will my breathing to calm and my
heart rate to regulate. The familiar tingling in my hands and
the lightness of my head cause me to find some way to
become grounded. I focus on Angel, describing the black cat
out loud and talking to her. My body slowly calms.

It's just a dream.

It's just a dream.

I hope it's just a dream.

Once I'm a little calmer, my furry roommate jumps the
space between my dresser and my bed. Climbing into my
lap, her head bumps into my hands. The feel of her soft fur
and the sound of her gentle purrs finish grounding me. This
cat is turning out to be more than a companion in my lonely
job. She watches over me and calms my raging emotions. I
don't know what I'd do without her.

After deciding sleep isn't happening anymore tonight, I
slide back against my headboard, cat curling up in my lap. I

grab my book. There are only a couple more chapters left, and there's plenty of time to finish it before the sun comes up. Tonight will be the night I discover who the killer is.

I'VE STARTED to get up early so I can take my showers in the morning, in the daylight. Although daylight has no place in this dark hall besides the small kitchen I rummaged around in for snacks last night. Too shook up to sleep, I had finished my book and fed Angel some cheese and crackers from my plate. She didn't seem to mind my company or the snacks.

Hair still wet, I pull it up in the bun that feels like it's sucking my brain out through my skull. I examine myself in the mirror, taking in my freshly made dress. While it can certainly use a bit of color, the seamstress did a great job. Smoothing my hands over my perfect-fitting dress, I move on to start my job.

MASTER RADCLIFFE IS another no-show this morning. I'm currently up to my elbows in greasy bubbles from another breakfast not eaten. Staring at two unused plates, I don't understand why I have to wash both. Every meal I have to wash the unused plate that sits next to Master Radcliffe, but at times like this, I have to wash two clean plates. It seems like overkill.

Once the breakfast is scrubbed off the pans, I grab the towel to dry them, cringing at the greasy feeling covering my hands and forearms. The counters are then wiped down and dried. Appliances must be made spotless too. Double-checking to ensure my work meets Gertrude's standards, I turn off the lights and exit the sparkling kitchen.

"Miss Blackwood!"

I hold back my groan. Has she just been standing here waiting for me? It would've been faster with help. I keep that thought to myself. "Yes, madame?"

"Master Radcliffe made a mess in the den last night." Turning, she walks away. *Why don't you clean it yourself?*

Once again keeping my inner thoughts to myself, I head to the closet to grab a cleaning cart. Lack of sleep has left me a little cranky, but I can't let it get me fired. Feeling some-one's gaze on the back of my neck in the empty darkness of the gloomy hallway, I quicken my pace. I never feel alone here, not in a good way. The eyes never feel friendly.

Hesitating, I poke my head into the den. The candles and taxidermy are still lined along the mantle over the fire-place. The demon ashtray lies on the carpet, cigar ashes spilled all over the place. That could've been from Master Radcliffe this time. A few books lay strewn carelessly on top of the couch.

Sighing, I grab the vacuum from the cart. I find the cigar butt under the vacant armchair, clean the ashes that have spilled from the ceramic ashtray, and place it back on the table with the old radio and lamp.

"Stay," I say, pointing at the ashtray. I think I'm definitely going insane. Did I just talk to the teleporting ceramic ashtray?

After vacuuming the spilled ashes, I return the vacuum to the cart and grab the books left on the couch, placing them on top of the cleaning supplies for transport to where they belong. Master Radcliffe has some interesting tastes. There must be many murder mysteries in this house. No wonder I have been spending so much time trying to solve murders in my room at night. I wonder if there's anything else in the library.

As I go to leave, a loud thud leaves me frozen at the door. My hand trembles, remembering the familiar noise. I know if I turn around, the ashtray will be on the floor. I can't look. Glancing down the dark halls, I see no one in view. I slip out the door, the click of the latch echoing in the eerie hallway.

It was on the table when I left.

Stopping at the library, I return the books to their proper shelves and turn to walk away. They fall back off, thudding on the thick rug beneath the shelves. After replacing them again, I make sure they are wedged tight enough to stay. Closing the door, I hear multiple thumps and pages rustle through the crack in the slightly opened door.

"Oh, hell no."

I close the door with a quick click, then start pushing my cart to finish the rest of my chores for the day. I'm not in the mood for dealing with strange objects falling again. My mind can't handle it today. Let's hope they don't follow me.

GERTRUDE HAD SENT me on an errand into town to restock Master Radcliffe's liquor cabinet after lunch. To my disappointment, I didn't meet a certain man that makes my heart flutter. Bottles clink as I place various types of whiskey in their rightful places, careful not to break any. I guess when you're reclusive in this dreary setting, drinking seems as good an entertainment as any. It's never been an activity I wish to indulge in.

"Dear Emma!"

I turn my head to see the portly cook enter the kitchen, a warm smile lighting up his face. "Enabling the Master's vices," he chuckles with a wink.

My giggle joins his chuckle. There is just something about this kind man that puts me at ease. He oozes with friendliness and cheer, a welcome reprieve from the darkness this place brings. Peter starts bustling around the kitchen, making another impressive mess for me to clean while cooking dinner. I don't even mind, glad for the company after another long night.

Baking some delectable-looking chicken, he shows me the fastest way to peel potatoes. I laugh as peels go flying, ignoring the fact I will have to clean them up later. After I arrange the plates on the serving cart, the clock strikes five, and Peter rushes out with a short farewell.

Master Radcliffe is sitting at the table, waiting for his meal with Gertrude at her usual post. I place his plate of food on his serving dish, sparing a quick glance at the empty place, still curious who it is set for when no one ever visits. I do my best to avoid his eyes as I squeeze a lemon into his water. With that done, I scurry to my place.

As I stand there, listening to my boss's silverware scraping his plate, my mind wanders. The scraping stops, causing me to glance at my employer. His disturbing, cold eyes are staring at me. My heart stops as I try to think if I missed something. Did I screw up? Did he say something?

Without a single word, Master Radcliffe goes back to his meal, and I breathe a quiet sigh of relief. I find his eyes on me multiple times when I glance at him. That distant stare creeps me out, but I try to hold back my shudder. Eventually, the disturbing man finishes his dessert and clicks his cane down the hallway.

After finding all the potato peelings I can, I wash dishes

and wipe down surfaces before heading to my room. Upon entering my cramped space, I release my red hair from its confining bun, reveling in my scalp's relief. With a sigh of respite, I glance around. My book sits on the nightstand. Guess now is a good time to find something new.

I make my way to the library.

CHAPTER EIGHT

Frozen Assets

Book in hand, I reach the bottom of the central staircase. I didn't think it was possible, but this place is even darker after hours. My anxiety picks up a few notches. The thought of the increased darkness makes me shiver. I've never been a jumpy person. Life is less scary than the death that assaults me in my dreams. What can the real world throw at me that's worse than dying in agony every night?

Opening the wooden door to the library, I notice a fire is crackling in the fireplace. I freeze when I see the figure sitting in the chair by the fire. Cold golden-brown eyes meet mine. My gaze drops quickly, looking anywhere but those disturbing eyes. "Sorry, Master Radcliffe. I didn't realize you were in here. I didn't mean to disturb you."

"Miss Blackwood?" My hands immediately become clammy at the sound of my name on his lips. His voice reminds me of sandpaper running over rough, uneven brick. Something about it makes my skin crawl like I'm covered in thousands of spiders.

"Yes, sir?" I try to sound calm and confident, but the slight tremor in my voice betrays my unease.

"I'd like something to warm my stomach," his voice grates as he turns a page in the book. "I would like a glass of bourbon, three cubes of ice."

"Yes, sir. Would you like anything else?"

Master Radcliffe grunts a no, and I scurry back out into the dark hall, tucking the book in the pocket of my apron. Anything to get away from my employer's attention. I make it to the kitchen without incident, breathing a loud sigh of relief. I grab the bottle of bourbon from the liquor cabinet. Opening the cupboard that holds the glasses, I stare at them with apprehension.

Which glass do I use? Master Radcliffe is not the kind of man who is happy when anything is out of place. Everything must be done in the exact way he wishes. He doesn't accept mistakes. Wracking my brain, I remember seeing movies where people drink this kind of alcohol in a short glass. Not knowing what else to do, I grab one of those and walk it over to the refrigerator.

I scream when I open the freezer, dropping the glass to shatter on the clean floor. The head of a woman with red hair rests within the cold confines of the freezer. Blood is frozen in streams across the bottom of the cold box of death. It splatters the sides, forming glistening crystals of crimson.

Her skin is covered in a blue-gray shade of cold death. Not all the blood I see comes from the severed and desiccated neck. A ragged wound along the forehead oozes crimson down over her stiff, lifeless face. Her bright red hair is darkened into an even darker shade of red, stiffened with the stickiness of the thick liquid. Frost covers every part of the head not coated in blood.

The head's blue eyes open, staring at me with agony deep in their brilliant depths. Even in the cloud of death, those bright blues are stunning. After a long blink, the mouth opens, trying to speak without a sound. Blood runs from its mouth and down the front of the refrigerator. Once the river of red reaches the floor, it slowly flows toward my feet. I jump back before it can reach me, another scream bellowing from deep within my chest.

"Miss Blackwood!" Gertrude stands in the doorway leading out into the hall. "What are you screaming about?"

I turn back to the freezer, ready to point, only to find it empty of everything but ice and food. My mouth drops open. I try to speak, but I can't. The words won't come. There is no sign of what I have just witnessed; no head, no blood, and not a single red hair. Nothing provides evidence that what I saw was anything but a hallucination.

I must be going crazy!

"I-I-I am sorry, madame," I stammer, still unable to believe the head is gone. "My mind must be playing tricks on me."

Gertrude grunts but doesn't look convinced. Eyes falling to the floor at my feet, she glares. "You broke a glass. You're not in here getting drunk, are you? Just because I sent you to buy it does not mean you can drink it."

"N-n-no, madame," I blurt out, frantic at the thought of upsetting my supervisor and still unsettled over what I just witnessed. "The master was in the library when I went to exchange a book. He asked me to get him a glass of bourbon."

Gertrude is eyeing my loose hair with distaste. At the mention of Master Radcliffe, her eyes go wide, and she enters panic mode. "Then what are you waiting for?!"

My mouth drops open. Gertrude rushes over to grab another glass, pouring the golden liquid over three ice cubes she retrieves from the freezer free of blood and death. She hands me the glass in haste. "Get going. I'll clean this up."

Ushering me from the kitchen, Gertrude rushes toward the cleaning closet, black bun swaying as she walks at a brisk pace. I make my way back to the library. My employer is still sitting in the same spot. Master Radcliffe doesn't even look up at my entrance, turning another page of his book. "What took so long?"

I place the glass on the small table beside him. "Sorry, sir. I had trouble finding what I needed," I lie.

Those golden-brown eyes turn my way again. There is a flash of something in those hypnotic, yet disturbing, eyes. It's gone before I can place it. His raspy voice reaches my ears again. "Your hair is down, Miss Blackwood."

I straighten quickly, grabbing my red locks and pulling them back behind my shoulder. "I'm sorry, Master Radcliffe. I'm off duty and took my bun out before I remembered I need to exchange a book I finished for a new one."

Those eyes stare at me, and before I know it, I am unable to turn away. My fists clench and unclench in my black dress. I can feel sweat beading on my scalp. All breathing stops. Even my heart is subdued beneath the icy stare of Master Radcliffe. The man oozes something that instills fear.

After a nerve-wracking moment, his gaze is back on his book. I feel a bit dizzy after he releases me from his entrancing stare. I try to speak, but my mouth only opens and closes. I mentally force my fingers to relax. Breathing resumes. I feel as if I've been splashed with cold water into full consciousness.

"Very well," he rasps in impatience. "Get your book."

"Thank you, sir."

I scurry over to the bookshelves, returning my murder mystery to the shelf from which it came. Perusing, I try to make a pick as fast as possible. "Second shelf, third book from the end closest to the outside wall."

That raspy voice makes me jump. *Get a hold of yourself, Emma.* "Excuse me, sir?"

"Second shelf, third book from the end." Master Radcliffe sounds like he doesn't like to repeat himself. I gulp before turning back toward the shelves of books.

I follow his instructions, pulling the book he directed me to from between the others. "I'm not really a romance reader, Master Radcliffe."

His chuckle sends shivers all over. If I think his voice makes me uncomfortable, his laughter is enough to make my blood run cold. "You'll like that one."

I'm not sure why he thinks he knows my taste in books, but I decide it isn't a good idea to argue with him. "Thank you for the recommendation, Master Radcliffe," I say, slipping the book into my pocket.

My employer only grunts, eyes not leaving his pages. Why is everyone grunting at me tonight? Have all the people in this house become cavemen? I don't deserve to be grunted at. Words are enough.

Without voicing my annoyance, I head to the door and open it. "Goodnight, Master Radcliffe."

I turn as I say my goodnight. His cold eyes meet mine again. My mouth goes dry. Master Radcliffe doesn't reply, only stares in silence. Feeling unnerved by his unwavering eyes, I bow my head and slip out the door. I press my back against the cool wood and take deep breaths. When my legs feel steady again, I straighten and walk toward the staircase.

Once in my room again, I change into my pajamas and slide under the covers, still shaking from the eventful trip downstairs. Angel joins me by curling up so tight against my leg, I feel we are almost one. Her purrs reach my ears as I run my hand over her soft black fur. The comforting sound further relaxes my tense muscles.

I glance at the cover of the book. A man and an overly enthusiastic woman are kissing, wrapped in each other's arms. The cover is faded, and the binding is heavily creased and cracked. "I really don't like romance, Angel."

Those yellow eyes look up at me, eyelids drooping. "I guess I can give it a shot. I'm not sure if he's going to ask about it," I tell her.

Her purrs reach the high pitch that I have come to believe she emits when happy with my attention. I smile, scratching along her chin. "What would I do without you?"

She stares at me for a few seconds before putting her head down, completing her perfect furry ball. I smile and flip to the first page of the well-used book. The cliché start makes me groan. Still, I continue on. Master Radcliffe may ask about it if I run into him outside the dining room again, not that I want to.

Looking at my phone, I realize it is midnight. I'm a few chapters in already. I guess this must be a different kind of romance because I became lost in it. No others have ever held my interest before. Romance usually doesn't last past the first chapter because I find the sappiness unrealistic. Confused by my reluctance, I mark my place and close the book before turning off my light.

ANGEL SHIFTING her position drags me out of my slumber before the terrifying nightmares can pull me under further. The black cat moves again, invisible in the darkness engulfing my room. "Will you stay still?"

Her low growl wakes me further. My heart begins to hammer in my chest. I can tell by her movements that she is crouched low. I don't need to see her to tell that her ears are flattened.

Please tell me she is just mad at me for moving or something.

After feeling the furry tail thrash against my face, I realize my guardian is facing that dreaded corner again. Thoughts of the dead woman in the bathroom and the bloody head in the freezer flash in my mind. I don't want to look. Angel's hisses turn urgent. My heart hammers in my chest, and my body begins to tremble.

I reach over to turn on my light, but it only flashes with a loud pop and sizzle. That is really bad timing. I'm not sure how much light will help, but I'll feel better with it. A false sense of security would be better than none right now. Grabbing my phone, I turn on its flashlight. The beam shakes as I slowly move it to light up the corner I don't want to see.

Golden-brown eyes gleam beneath a black top hat, shining in my light. He doesn't even react to the brightness pointed directly at his face. They're still cold, but they look pleased as well. The light from my phone gives his face an eerie glow that causes my hand to shake even more. Holding back a scream, I sit up quickly, displacing the cat still hissing at my side.

I have never seen Master Radcliffe smile, and I can't say it's something I ever want to see again. He's obviously happy, but there's a deviousness to that smile that makes my hair stand on end. Feeling at a disadvantage, I slowly climb out of my bed, light never leaving the corner. My legs threaten to buckle, but I manage to stay upright.

"M-M-Master Radcliffe," I stutter, inching backward.

He doesn't reply, only taps his cane on the wooden floor.

I flinch at the sound echoing in the confines of my otherwise silent room. Cool metal reaches my fingers. I twist the doorknob before flinging the door open. I blink at the intrusion of the light from the hall, trying to adjust to its dim, yet flooring, brightness.

The corner is empty.

CHAPTER NINE

Bonus

I lick the last of the cream cheese from my bagel off my fingers as I turn another page. After grabbing my book and phone, I have not returned to my room. There is just no way I can make myself go back so soon after my employer appeared and disappeared from that blasted corner. What is it about that corner?

Surely, I must have been dreaming last night. Master Radcliffe can't just appear and disappear when he wants. Despite how logical that sounds, I can't get the creepy look out of my mind. He seemed very satisfied with something, and I really don't want to know what. Nothing about Master Radcliffe instills warmth and trust.

One thing that is good about not being able to sleep, I've made it through most of the book. I meant what I said to my boss; romance is not my thing. I'm not sure what it is about this one, but I absolutely cannot put it down. There's a sense of mystery and adventure mixed in with the romance of the plot. Maybe that's it.

As I turn to take a drink of milk, soft fur touches my fingers. I place the glass down, then notice Angel has jumped up on the table and is now laying across my open book. Laughing, I stroke her black fur, releasing a loud purr from the golden-eyed cat on the table.

"I was reading that," I laugh.

Angel closes her big round eyes, ignoring my need for

book closure. Smiling, I lift my phone and notice it is time to get moving anyway. Once I stand, she hops off the table and runs back to my room. Looking around, I slowly slip into my room, wary of what may be hiding in the dim space. Nothing jumps out of the creepy corner as I lay my book down on my nightstand, grab a work dress, and walk to the bathroom.

Steam covers everything when I step out of my rejuvenating shower. I wrap the towel around me and walk over to the mirror. My freckled face comes into view as I clean the fog from the mirror, skin pink from the hot water. I dry myself, paying special attention to my thick red hair.

After sliding my dress over my head, I turn back to the mirror to find it fogged up again. I run my hand across it. When my palm reaches the bottom, I hear a loud crack and jump back with a squeal. A line forms from the top right corner to the bottom left, inching across the shiny surface. The crack in the glass turns dark red. My hand flies to my mouth as the red begins to trickle slowly down the mirror in streams of crimson.

My hands shake, and I back up toward the door one small step at a time. The mirror drips blood from the crack like it is a vicious wound. It drips onto the floor. Instead of pooling on the tile, it snakes my way, finally causing me to let out a full-blown scream. Frantic, I grab for the doorknob and run straight into Gertrude on the other side of the door.

"Emma! What do you think you're doing? Why are you screaming?"

Pointing, I turn to the bathroom, only to drop my hand in shock. The mirror is whole, not a single blemish. There is no blood anywhere as if nothing ever happened. My bottom lip trembles. I'm not crazy. I can't be.

"I-I-I'm sorry, madame. I haven't been sleeping well, and I must have been seeing things."

The black bun turns to the side as she cocks her head at me. Gertrude seems skeptical as she looks at me with narrowed, dark eyes. So quick I jump, her eyes dart into the bathroom, and the suspicious look she was giving me turns into a glare. I try to follow her gaze but don't see anything that would warrant that intense staredown.

My supervisor turns back to me, glare replaced with an emotionless expression. "I have placed your first week's pay on the stand beside your bed. What made you choose that book?"

I clear my throat, trying to ignore the strange exchange Gertrude made with empty air. "Master Radcliffe suggested it after I gave him his bourbon last night."

A look I can't decipher glitters in her eyes. I can't decide if it is a good look or a bad one, but she remains silent for a while before shaking her head. With the snootiness back in her voice, she says, "Master Radcliffe is pleased with your work so far. He has given you a bonus. The master prefers to pay in cash, so do with it as you will. He has also given you the day off."

Without waiting for a reply, she turns and walks away, black bun bobbing down the hall. I look down at my dress and sigh. I am definitely not going out in this, but at least she told me before I put my hair in that awful bun. I swear if I keep pulling my hair that tight, I'm going to go bald. That wouldn't be a good look for me.

Running down the hall, I open the window in the servant's kitchen and stick my head out to gauge the weather. It is bright, sunny, and warm. After returning to my room, I throw on a pair of shorts and a nicer-looking tee shirt that hugs my curves. It'll be nice to have a day out of that formal black dress.

AFTER HANGING up the receiver of the payphone, I lean against the glass of the booth with a sigh. I miss Ava, and it is clear she misses me. There's no way I could go visit her with my unpredictable schedule, and I don't dare invite her here. That seems like it would be an incredibly bad idea.

The door screeches as I open it to find a pair of golden-brown eyes staring back at me. I can't stop the smile that stretches over my face. Those striking eyes look me up and down real quick, and the look on his face makes me blush. I chose my outfit well. After exchanging greetings, we begin a little tour.

Edgar takes me to a small park found behind the local businesses. We sit by a fountain with an angel holding a bowl of flowing water while he shows me a picnic basket that he stashed when he saw me leaving the mansion. We have a nice picnic next to the sound of trickling water, full of smiles and laughter. There is just something about this alluring man that draws me to him. He and Angel are my only light in this dark place.

After our meal, we walk along the sidewalks again, Edgar smiling and talking to everyone we meet. Some still look at me with a little apprehension or hope, but most are friendly when I am with the town's golden boy. We enter the seamstress shop, the owner looking up as the bell rings upon our entrance.

She smiles at Edgar, but the smile falls when she sees me. "Does Master Radcliffe need another order?"

The apprehension in her voice makes me sigh. That man sits in his mansion on top of the town, and everyone within view is terrified of him. "No," I answer her, watching the relieved smile stretch her lips. "I saw you have other clothes here and wanted to look around."

Her smile brightens. "Of course!"

Edgar follows me as I peruse the shelves and racks. "Does nothing please you?"

I take in his jeans and polo shirt. "Where do you get your clothes?"

He laughs, golden-brown eyes twinkling. "I order them. Everything in this town is...."

"Outdated?"

Edgar laughs again, and I feel myself being hypnotized by that glorious sound. "The people in this town are pretty isolated and old-fashioned."

"I noticed. Oh! That's pretty."

I walk over to a dress that is on a mannequin in the back. It looks unfinished, but the turquoise dress is somewhere in between modern and old-fashioned. My hand runs over the fabric, marveling at how soft it is. Simple, the dress hugs and hangs in all the right places, a braided black belt circling around the waist. It's a beautiful and unique dress.

"Do you like it?" Edgar sounds sad, so I turn.

"I do. Why are you so sad?"

Those entrancing eyes settle on my face, grief and longing moistening them. "It was being made for someone special. She disappeared, and it waits for her return."

My brows furrow, and I turn back to the dress, wondering why this town is so lost in its memories. I get the feeling something bad happened here. Not wanting to upset him more, I go back to browsing through the clothes on the racks. In the end, I find a couple of blouses and skirts that won't make me look like a grandma and walk up to pay.

Edgar offers to pay as I pull out my wallet. "No thank you," I say. "I got paid today and managed to earn a bonus. Besides, I don't want you always spending money on me."

"A bonus," the handsome man says. "I guess you do a great job. That is actually a good sign."

Handing the seamstress some cash, I catch her hiding a look of hope. Before I can inquire about it, Edgar takes the bag from her and pulls me out of the shop. I sigh. "Why is that a good sign? Does he not give bonuses often?"

A guarded look crosses Edgar's features, and he runs his hand through his dark hair. "It's just... None of the other girls in your position usually last very long."

"They quit?"

He purses his lips. "I guess you could say they were fired. Master Radcliffe is very particular."

"Oh," I reply, my mouth remaining open as I take in what he says.

The master of the house rarely even acknowledges my presence unless he needs something. Maybe it's my silence and obedience that make him happy with my service. I've never been particularly well-liked by employers, usually late and anxious due to my terrifying recurring nightmare. Living in the manor has helped me avoid the late part, but something about that house seems off. I'd like to think it is all my imagination, yet too much is happening to make me believe it is all coincidence.

"Have the ghosts been behaving?"

I jump at his voice intruding in my thoughts. Yep, definitely still anxious. That part hasn't changed. The fact that his questions match what I'm thinking is not lost on me. "What?"

He smiles. "Last time, you asked me if the place is haunted."

My cheeks begin to burn. Not wanting to make him think less of me, I don't confide in him. I try to laugh, but it sounds hollow to my ears. "They seem to be."

Edgar's smile falls. "I'm sorry if I offended you. It wasn't my intention."

"No! It's fine."

He doesn't look convinced but doesn't push the matter as we return to the gate of the manor. "Well, this is where we must part, sweet Emma. I have duties to attend to."

Edgar takes my hand, his lips making it tingle. I say my goodbyes, wishing I could spend more time with him. Once inside the gate, I turn to watch him leave. The handsome man turns, raising his hand in a wave. I return it as the gates swing closed with a screech, my bag swinging with the momentum of my hand.

Dread washes over me as I turn to face the house.

CHAPTER TEN

Playing Pool

Laying in my bed, I manage to finish the book recommended by my boss. This is the fastest I have ever finished a book, but now I need something else to read. Checking the clock on my phone, I decide I have enough time to return the book and grab a new one before I find something to eat for supper. As I walk down the main staircase, I meet my employer walking up.

My eyes immediately drop to the dark carpet over the stairs as I mutter a greeting. Master Radcliffe doesn't answer, and I risk looking at him. Those disturbing eyes are fixated on the book in my hands. I can't stop fidgeting under his gaze. I'm ready for this meeting to end.

"Did you finish it?" His eyes never leave the book.

I run my teeth over my bottom lip. "Yes, sir. I really enjoyed it and couldn't put it down. Thank you for suggesting it."

A smile twitches at the corner of his lips. "You may keep that one in your room if you like. There is no need to return it to get another. I insist you keep it."

I open my mouth, but Master Radcliffe is already moving on. Reaching the library, I decide to keep the book in my hands but find another one as well. An interesting title catches my eyes, and I pull a book off the shelf. As soon as I see it is horror, I shove it back on the shelf and move on. I will not read horror in this house. Finding an interesting-looking adventure, I head back to my room and place both books on my stand before heading to the kitchen down the hall.

Opening the fridge, I see it freshly stocked with food. I have no idea where this comes from, but 'Madame' Gertrude has told me to eat whatever is in this room. A square of foil catches my eyes, and I pull it out. As I see the note written on it, I can't help but smile as the mystery is solved. Excitement overwhelms me.

The waitress at my diner says you really like grilled cheese. I made this special for you. I hope you enjoy the food I deliver for your kitchen. -Peter

That man is one of the sweetest people I have ever met. Thanks to the sadness that comes with watching so much of his food go to waste, I'm excited to get to eat something handmade specially for me. After heating the toaster oven, I slide the sandwich in to warm it and find a container of tomato and basil soup in the fridge. While the sandwich heats, I cook the soup in the microwave.

Sitting at the table, my mouth waters at the smell of the food in front of me. I take a bite of the gooey grilled cheese, moaning in pleasure. Each bite tastes like a piece of heaven. No wonder Peter is so popular. Angel appears by my chair.

"I have always loved grilled cheese, but this is simply amazing," I mumble. I laugh at her startled look when I hit her with crumbs while talking. After swallowing, I continue talking to the cat. "I don't know what he does, but somehow he is a grilled cheese god."

I dip the sandwich in the soup, and flavor bursts on my taste buds. No wonder the master has Peter cook his meals. If he can make a simple meal like this taste as if it came from heaven, I can only imagine the more sophisticated dishes I see him make for my boss. I savor every bite.

My alarm wakes me from my slumber. For once, my night was dreamless and free of creepiness. Angel purrs as I scratch her soft fur, giving me a chirp of happiness while she snuggles against me.

"I'm sorry, my warm ball of fur, but I need to get up. No day off today."

The black cat breathes an annoyed sigh as I slide from the covers. I grab my dress and head to the bathroom. Staring at the mirror, I'm afraid to do much of anything in this room today. With a quick sniff, I decide I will do with a face wash and brushing of my teeth. Once that is done, I slip my dress on and tie my bun as tight and perfect as possible while standing back away from the mirror.

When I reach the bottom floor, Gertrude tells me that Master Radcliffe is not eating breakfast and gives me a list of my duties for the day. After going over my schedule, I sigh at the amount I have to do today. Gertrude and her bun of perfection are already gone, so I grab my cleaning cart and begin my day. With so much to do, it's better not to procrastinate.

My first assignment is the billiard room. Upon entering, it turns out that this room may actually be a quick clean. I marvel at the fact that this house has a fireplace in every single room and can't help but wonder who keeps the fires tended. Isaac, maybe?

With a shrug, I examine the area I need to clean. The center of the dark hardwood floor is covered by an equally dark red carpet. Red couches line the walls paneled in wood. The pool table sits in the center of the red carpet, its green velvet looking almost new, only marred in a few places. The balls are set up, ready for a game.

It probably is nearly new. I have yet to see a guest here in this giant mansion of a house. The scars look old, which doesn't surprise me. I've never seen anyone but the creepy man and his servants in this house. How much space does one aging man need?

Maybe Master Radcliffe wasn't always alone. Everyone has family and people they love, don't they? My mind wanders, thinking of what might be in my employer's past. Maybe something bad happened to turn him into the grouchy man he is today. Maybe he was born like this.

Sighing, I realize I will never get the answers to any of my questions. Gertrude has forbidden snooping, and it is clear that Master Radcliffe is a very secretive man. Even Edgar won't answer my questions straight out. That surprises me, seeing how open Edgar is with me. Maybe it's so terrible that no one wants to speak of it. When considering how depressed and scared the town seems, I would think that is very likely. It is like the town is caught in a fog of despair that no one has the ability to lift.

With another sigh, I begin my task. The only light is the one over the pool table, leaving the room eerie and dark. Unsure how to tell if a dark carpet is clean in the low light, I sweep and vacuum it all after dusting. I bend down to unplug the vacuum cleaner, then jump up and spin to face the table. My heart's in my throat.

The balls still sit in perfect formation on the table, the solids and stripes alternating in their triangle. The white ball rests at the other end, waiting for someone to propel it toward the colors. Everything is as it should be. My brows furrow, and I shake my head. I could have sworn I heard...

Get it together, Emma. You're just hearing things.

I breathe out the next sigh and bend down to wrap the cord around the brackets meant to hold it. The sound of pool balls clacking echoes in the room again, making me squeal and jump. All balls are still where they should be. My hands shake, my heart rate increasing with labored breaths. I know what I heard. I've played pool with Ava at the local bar many times. That is a break I heard.

Licking my lips, I look around nervously for any sign of where the sound came from. Nothing in the room is out of place, and my shaking only increases with that realization. In a hurry to get out of this room, I put the vacuum on the cart. Just as I push the cleaning cart through the door, I hear a high-pitched giggle and low chuckle. The hair on the back of my neck stands on end, and I bolt out of the room, slamming the door behind me.

As I hurry to turn the corner, I hear someone yell. I skid to a stop, barely managing to keep the cart from slipping out of my fingers to continue down the hall by itself. Isaac pokes his blond head around the corner, blue eyes wide. I almost took out the groundskeeper.

"I'm so sorry!" It seems I'm going to find some way to get myself into trouble.

Isaac gives me a big grin. "It's fine, Emma. Just scared the daylights out of me. Actually, maybe you can help me, now that you are done trying to pull off a hit-and-run with your cart. I'd rather ask you than Gerty."

It is hard not to giggle at his pet name for his coworker. "What do you need?"

"I made quite a mess with oil out in the shed. Do you know if we have any extra dish soap?"

"Actually, each cart has a bottle, just in case. You can have this one, and I'll make a mental note to restock it when I return the cart."

I bend down to open the cabinet in the cart and pull out a large container of dish soap. "Thank you, Emma. You're a lifesaver," Isaac says.

I smile, handing the cleaner to Isaac, but the smile dies as I notice that he is staring at my eyes again. Blinking a few times, I try to dislodge his stare without success. "Do you need something else, Isaac?"

The blond man shakes his head, releasing me from his gaze. "No. Thank you for this. I just can't get over how your eyes are such a rare color, the perfect blend of blue and green."

I stammer for something to say, but the unnerving man turns and walks down the dim hallway. Every time I meet Isaac, it seems he becomes stranger and stranger. I'm starting to wonder if I should wear sunglasses when he's around. His obsession with my eyes makes me uncomfortable.

CHAPTER ELEVEN

Permanent Records

The smell of lemon cleaning solution fills the air as I run a soft cloth over the railing of the master staircase to remove the dust from it. After eradicating every speck of dust, I run a different cleaner over the rail to preserve the expensive dark wood and make it gleam in the low light of the chandelier above. I wonder how this place would look in bright light. Once the railing is as sparkly as possible, I grab the vacuum and start running over the carpet.

"This thing is heavy," I grunt between gritted teeth as I move it from one step to the next. It shouldn't surprise me that they'd have an old, heavy vacuum instead of the lighter equipment from a more modern time. We can't spend any of our vast wealth to help the servants out, can we?

The fibers of the dark carpet shift back and forth as I suck all the dirt out of it. Remembering Gertrude's lessons, I make sure that each one is left the same way to ensure no vacuuming lines can be spotted. A stubborn string manages to avoid being picked up by the brushes. Bending down, I pick at it and pull, wincing at the tearing sound that follows. I kneel and examine the carpet closer, noticing that it is scuffed and worn at the edge and coming up from the hardwood it used to be fastened to.

I chew my lip, trying to think of what to do. There's no way my pull caused this much damage. Standing, I extract a little pad out of the cart and write the damaged carpet down, including which step, what side, and leaving out my little addition to the damage. Gertrude has told me that any damaged property needs to be recorded, so it can be properly inspected. Damage is an eyesore Master Radcliffe will not tolerate.

The sound of the vacuum begins again, and my fingers tingle with the constant vibrations. I can't help but think again that a man with Master Radcliffe's means should be able to afford a more modern vacuum or two. By the time I reach the top of the stairs, sweat is beading my forehead, and my breaths come out in ragged pants. My head is beginning to ache with how loud this monstrosity is. At least I'm done with it for now.

With a big sigh of relief, I place the vacuum in its upright position and stop to breathe for a moment. My eyes travel down the darker hallway to my left. My teeth find my bottom lip again as I stare down the forbidden hallway. What is down that dark passageway that I am not allowed to see? What deep, dark secrets lay hidden down that hall?

I know Master Radcliffe's rooms are down there, but multiple doors line the walls from what I can see from this vantage point. My curious mind wonders what's behind those doors. My imagination runs wild and not in a good way. Chills run along my spine, making me shiver as I look into the darkness in front of me. Do I even want to know what lies hidden down there?

"Miss Blackwood?"

I nearly scream as my hand reaches for my racing heart while I spin to confront my source of fright. Gertrude stands behind me, her arms crossed and staring with a stern look on her face, not a strand of hair out of place. "Yes, madame?"

"What are you doing?"

Looking down, I smooth a non-existent wrinkle from my dress and give a fake cough. "Nothing, madame. I was just taking a breather after cleaning the staircase."

"You better not be thinking of going down that hall."

I shake my head so hard my tight bun pulls at my scalp. "I'm not, madame. I swear."

Her dark eyes peer at me from below her tight bun. "Make sure you don't. Are you doing your chore list in order?"

"Yes, madame."

"And this is all the further you've gotten?"

My breath stops. I had no idea I was being timed. At my pace, I would have no trouble finishing at the end of my shift, so I didn't think I needed to hurry. "Sorry, madame. I was trying to pace myself and make sure everything was as clean as possible before moving on. I will be finished by the end of the day."

That hard stare makes me squirm. "Maybe you wouldn't be so far behind if you hadn't been playing pool?"

My mouth drops open. "What?"

"Why were the pool balls all over the table? I had to fix them. Master Radcliffe likes everything in their proper place."

My eyes widen. "I don't know what you are talking about, madame. I cleaned the room and left. When I closed the door, they were in their proper place, not all over the table."

Dark eyes narrow. "I'm pretty sure no one else was in there today, Miss Blackwood."

"I swear!"

"This will go on your record. Please stay on task from now on. I will take over what is next on your list. There is an errand you need to run."

There's a record? Is this like the permanent record in school? But I didn't do anything. Despite my strong desire to argue, I feel my mouth will only get me into more trouble. When Gertrude moves her hand, I realize she has a garment bag in it. I was so consumed with everything she was saying that I never noticed it before now.

Gertrude hands me the bag. "Take this to the seamstress. Master Radcliffe made a bit of a mess on it, and she is the only one who knows how to get it out. Do not look in the bag."

I grab the hanger as she thrusts it in my direction. Before I can ask any questions, the vacuum is overwhelming the once silent staircase as the black bun bobs with the force of her pushing it back and forth across the carpet. Without more hesitation, I drape the bag over my shoulder and head toward the front door. I won't argue with a chance to get out of this dreary house.

The wind hits me as soon as I walk through the gate. There is a chill in the breeze today, probably due to the sun hiding behind dark clouds. The scent of moisture hangs in the air, and I hope that it doesn't rain before I can make my way back. I start down the lane, making sure the bag does not drag along the dirt of the road. I don't need another black mark on whatever record Gertrude keeps. Is it for Master Radcliffe or just for her need for control?

The streets are nearly empty as I walk toward the familiar shop. The owner looks up as I enter, taking in my bun and work attire. "Does the master need something?"

Sliding the bag over the counter, I explain that my employer made a mess that needs to be cleaned off his suit. She sighs and hangs the bag on the rack behind her. "I'll have it done by tomorrow. Do your dresses fit alright?"

I nod but refrain from telling her that they really aren't

my style. A rumble of thunder makes me glance out the shop window at the quickly darkening sky. "Do I need to do anything else?"

She shakes her head. "It'll be added to his account. You better get going before the skies open up on you."

Before turning to the door, I send her another quick nod. As I exit, I risk one last glance behind me. She is opening the bag but sees me looking and zips it back up quickly. I see the mess all over the garment inside before it's hidden from view again. My mouth falls open, the threat of rain forgotten.

She looks nervous, eyes shifting back and forth. "Do you need anything else, Emma?"

I shake my head in answer and hurry out the door. That can't be what I think it is. Maybe it's wine. That's not right. I have never seen him drink wine, only whiskey. There's no way that would be blood, would it? It can't be.

My steps carry me toward the house overlooking the tiny town, but my mind never leaves the shop. I pause, fear taking over as I decide that was most definitely blood. Fingers trembling, I walk with hesitant steps. When I'm about halfway back, another peal of thunder shakes the air, and big drops begin to hit the top of my head.

The stains forgotten, I begin to jog back to the house but don't even make the gate before the water comes in what feels like bucketfuls. Water pelts me so hard that I feel I may be knocked down and swept away. By the time I enter the front door, gasping for breath, every single part of me is soaked. I dash up to the servant's quarters, changing as fast as possible and adjusting my bun.

Once presentable, I walk back down the stairs in search of my supervisor. I still cannot get those red stains out of my mind, but I know better than to ask Gertrude. She gave me specific orders not to look. Did he hurt himself? Is someone else hurt? Who's blood is it?

I check the library first, only to find it spotless and devoid of the black bun. Two more chores down the list, and I find Gertrude in the dining room, just finishing up. Without a word, she pushes me the cart and walks out of the room, into the dim hall. After checking my list, I follow her out. Next, I need to clean the hall floors and walls. Gertrude is at the end of the hall when I feel something hit me hard.

Crying out, I fall against the wall. Within seconds, Gertrude is beside me. "Did you trip?"

"No, madame. I feel like someone pushed me."

She shakes her head. "No one else is here, Miss Blackwood."

"I know. I just..."

Her dark eyes narrow again. "Did you consume alcohol while you were out? I will not stand having a drunk under my supervision."

"No! I just dropped off the suit and came straight back."

"Let me smell your breath?"

What? Is she crazy? She can't be serious. Her cold stare makes me comply. Gertrude looks thoughtful after I breathe in her face, watching me with suspicious eyes. "You're lucky. I didn't smell any alcohol or a breath mint to cover it up."

Gertrude turns and walks away before I can answer. I rub the part of my arm that felt like it was hit. Pain makes me wince. Walking into the downstairs bathroom, I unzip my dress and pull the arm down. A red mark that looks a good bit like a handprint is already darkening into a bruise. I begin to shake, unable to control my trembling.

I didn't imagine this one.

CHAPTER TWELVE

Laundry Day

The steam created by the shower soothes my tired eyes. I close them, trying to stop the burning left over from yet another sleepless night. Even the energizing scent of my body wash cannot wake me up. After last night, dreams of my employer covered in blood haunted me, replacing my usual nightmare. In some dreams, he was gravely injured, but most were much more sinister in nature. I blame my dreams on the visions of Master Radcliffe in the corner of my room and the stains on his suit.

Slowly opening the shower curtain, I peek around it at the empty bathroom. Nothing spooky is in sight, but that doesn't mean I can let my guard down. I step out onto the soft, fuzzy mat and grab my towel. The brush glides through my long hair, stopping its trail through my thick locks as I untangle the knots left from my restless sleep and scrubbing. Once my hair is in its annoying bun, I finish drying and slip my dress on.

Before sliding my arm into the sleeve, I examine the hand-shaped bruise on my skin with a shudder. My hopes that everything is my imagination are shattered with the appearance of this bruise. I shake my head. No, surely I just ran into something and the bruise just resembles a hand out of coincidence. That's got to be it. With a sigh, I leave to start my day.

I STUFF the linens Gertrude has left for me into the washing machine. Today is laundry day, and I am slipping a few of my leisure clothes in with the manor's dirty items. I made sure to ask *madame* first and was surprised to have her allow it. A laundromat isn't something I've seen around town, so I guess there's not much choice but to let me clean my clothes. I'm sure even my leisure clothes aren't allowed to be dirty.

My duty entails sitting in the laundry room while everything is washed and dried to ensure nothing stops or leaks. Once the washing machine begins cycling, I sit in an uncomfortable wooden chair along the bland tan wall and pull out the adventure book I have been working on. This will be one of my easy jobs, and I look forward to catching up on my reading. The noisy machine stops after a little over three chapters.

I ready the load of towels I will be doing next, walk over to the washing machine, and reach for the soggy linens within. Instead of the soft feeling of cloth, my hand hits something round and firm. Curious, I pull my hand out and stare in horror at the crimson coating it. My entire body shakes as I gaze at the red running down my arm and dripping off my elbow. My breath stops as I cautiously look into the machine.

There are no linens in the washer. Body parts fill the round chamber, sticky liquid bubbling beneath them. Dismembered arms and legs fill the machine halfway. My mouth opens and closes in horror, which only intensifies as the blood beneath the body parts starts to rise. Unable to move, my feet remain rooted in the floor in front of the machine as the red liquid engulfs the appendages and continues to reach for the top of the washing machine. Bile rises in my throat.

As the blood reaches the top, I am finally able to dislodge my stuck feet and move backward, one small step at a time. I trip and fall, landing with a loud thump on the hardwood floor. I continue to back up, my hand leaving a trail of blood as I push myself backward. Crimson flows over the top of the open washer, cascading down the side in a demented waterfall, and spreading out in a dark red pool. It reaches for me, covering everything it touches. My heart hammers against my breastbone.

My back hits the closed door. As the blood flows closer, I begin to tremble and scream out in terror. When the crimson liquid is mere inches from my shaking body, I close my eyes tight and stop breathing. I risk forcing an eye open after a few moments, then both fly open in shock. The blood is gone. Raising my hand in front of my face, I see there is no blood on it anymore. Even my trail across the floor is gone.

I sit and shake for a while, unable to move as my mind races. My breathing becomes quick and harsh, outpaced by my racing heart. Once I slowly calm, I'm able to pry myself off the floor and take shaky steps toward the washing machine. It takes every bit of willpower I have to look into the washer, and I'm shocked to see clean linens instead of bloody limbs.

With reluctance, I reach in and wrap my trembling fingers around the cloth, pulling it out to examine. When I find no blood, I breathe deep and move the wet linens into the dryer with shaking hands. Once the next load is started, I sit in the chair but choose to watch the machines with strained eyes instead of my book. Each time a load is done, I am almost too terrified to look, but the blood and dismembered body parts never return. I'm going crazy. That's the only explanation for everything that is happening. I have to be going crazy.

Maybe Ava is right, and my lack of sleep is pushing me to the edge again.

THE SUN IS BEGINNING its descent by the time I leave, and the screeching gate closes behind me. The fog that surrounds this tiny town begins to roll down the hills, approaching the street like some kind of creeping omen. Not liking that thought, shivers run over me, and I quicken my pace. My work dresses are draped over my shoulder, weighing me down as my shoes squish in the mud still left from the rain that saturated everything yesterday.

Breathe, Emma. Your lack of sleep is only playing tricks on you. Remember what happened last time?

I shake my head, refusing to let the memories come forward again. There is no way I want to relive that. As I enter the town, I force the thoughts out of my head and pay closer attention to the shop signs, looking for anywhere that might sell medication. Sometimes, sleeping meds will help me sleep through the dreams, at least for a while. I'll take any help I can get right now.

When I reach the seamstress shop, I enter with a sigh. The woman behind the counter looks up, sending me a nervous smile. I swing the dresses off my shoulder and onto the counter. "Gertrude told me I can have these cleaned on Master Radcliffe's account."

"Of course!" She removes the dresses from the counter

and puts them on the racks behind her. "Master Radcliffe's suit is taking a bit longer than usual. Please assure him that it will be done tomorrow."

Fear makes her voice quiver, and I suppress the shudder at the red stains I saw yesterday. What is it about this man that puts these people on edge like this? Sure, he's a bit creepy, but I haven't seen anything that deserves this kind of terror. Unless it has something to do with the stains. I shake my head. No, that's a crazy thought. He probably just cut himself shaving.

"I'm sure it will be fine," I say.

Her eyes dart back and forth. "You're probably right."

I chew my bottom lip, not believing her words. Despite her affirmation, I can tell she doesn't believe it. Her voice shakes, as do her hands. The poor woman is on the verge of tears. There's also a sense of resignation somewhere in her manner.

"These will be done in a few days," she tells me, clearly looking to end the conversation.

Not wanting to think more about it, I take the cue and exit the tiny shop. The sun is a little closer to the tops of the hills sheltering this antique town, but I need to find some sleeping pills. I know there isn't anything the way I came, so I turn deeper into town. A scream escapes my lungs as I turn to meet someone standing right behind me.

Golden-brown eyes twinkle in amusement. "You scare too easy."

No one in the street stops to even look at the woman who released a blood-curdling scream. "Why do you always sneak up on me?"

Edgar laughs. "You just get too lost in your own head. I was walking normal."

With a blush, I look down and curse my plain jeans and

baggy shirt. It has been a long day, and all I had wanted before leaving the manor was to get out and get back as fast as possible. I never even thought I'd run into someone whose opinion I care about. I have two quests in this mission; clean dresses and sleep aid. Edgar didn't even cross my mind while I was getting ready.

I clear my throat. "Do you have a pharmacy here?"

Those entrancing eyes stare in question. I babble on, "I've been having trouble sleeping and am looking for something to help."

"Ah," he says. "Follow me. I can't stay long, but I can lead you there."

"What do you do that you are always busy?" I hurry to keep up, and he slows down so I can match his pace without gasping for air.

"A little of this; a little of that. Being the town golden boy is exhausting. I hope everything is alright. What is keeping you from sleeping?"

I lick my lips and decide to keep my fragile mental state to myself. "I'm not sure. It might just be nerves."

Edgar nods, and I breathe a sigh of relief when he asks no more. Soon we are in front of a tiny store. "We don't have anywhere that sells just medicine, but Mister Wilkins should have what you are looking for. I need to go, sweet Emma. I hope to see you soon."

After accepting a soft kiss on my hand, I watch him walk away, wishing I could spend more time with him. With a deep breath, I turn away and enter the store. A brass bell rings as I open the door, and a tall man with gray hair greets me with a smile. Come to think of it, besides Edgar, I haven't really seen too many younger people here. That thought sparks my interest, but my wonderings are interrupted.

Mister Wilkins stares at me with concern. "Are you okay, miss?"

I smile and assure him I am. I need to better control myself. The whole town doesn't need to know that I'm crazy. Once I figure out where the medicine is kept, I walk over to search the shelves. Not many of these brands are recognizable to me, but I eventually find what I am looking for. The sky is getting darker when I exit the little store, brown paper bag in hand, and I hasten my steps. I'm anxious to make it back to my current residence before dark.

Not that I feel entirely safe there either.

A light mist creeps onto the road, surrounding my hurrying feet. The fog gets closer, and my anxiety increases. I try to tell myself to be logical because it is only fog, but my reasoning doesn't slow my steps. The mist moves like it's alive. My mind thinks it looks hungry, and I curse my imagination for putting that thought into my brain.

I begin to shake as the gate comes into sight, but I tell myself the shapes I keep seeing in the rolling clouds are only my imagination and tricks of the light. Just as I reach the iron gates that strangely feel safer, something grabs my ankle, causing me to fall into the thickening mist covering the hardening mud on the ground. I cry out. With everything I have, I try to stand, but it feels as if I'm being held down.

Strange sounds reach my ears as hands grab at me. Grunts, snarls, and laughter echo in the thick air, an occasional scream reaching me through the clouds crawling along the ground. I fight as hard as I can, finally managing to crawl through the gate and hit the button to close it. My bag is on the other side, and I quickly reach through the gate to grab my medicine. As I pull my hand back, a tendril of fog curls around my wrist, but it feels like it is much more than mist. With one last loud cry, I scramble back and run for the house that looms against the dark sky, only a darker shadow in the increasing darkness. I don't even hesitate as I run through the front door. I'd rather face what's in the mansion than what's in the fog.

CHAPTER THIRTEEN

Drugged Sleep

The cool plastic cylinder in my hands feels good, but I am reluctant to start sleeping pills again. Ever since I was little, my parents and doctors have been thrusting medication into my hands, telling me the only thing I can do is force sleep and talk to people. No one understands what it feels like to be dependent on medicine to sleep. No one understands how it feels to bounce from psychiatrist to psychiatrist and be made to feel like I'm insane. No one understands how terrible I feel from night after night of drug-induced sleep.

No one even tries to understand why I don't want to do this. How is it so hard for others to be sympathetic to the fact that I don't want to live life in a medically induced fog? It consumes everything. I don't want to live like that again, but I can't live at all without better sleep. There's no true balance.

A short meow sounds beside me, but I don't look down. Purrs follow as a soft, furry head forces its way under my hand. Her insistence makes my eyes follow the comforting sound until I reach golden orbs framed in a pitch-black face. Those beautiful eyes stare up at me with pure and unconditional adoration, love only an animal can express. Love that I need more than anything right now. The cat doesn't understand what I'm going through, but she cares.

I sigh. "Angel, what am I going to do? I moved away

because I felt a new start, without people pushing doctors and pills on me, was what I needed to feel better. And here I am, sitting on a bed in a dreary room, holding a bottle of pills."

This was to be my fresh start. No more meddling parents. No more quack doctors. No more guilt from Ava's worried eyes. Somehow, the darkness has followed me. I'm sitting here contemplating returning to the things I hate for some relief.

"I have to do something." Her head bumps against my hand again, causing me to scratch without thought, purrs increasing in volume. "If I don't..."

I pause. Memories come flooding back, the last time I fought and lost control. I put the bottle on the stand by my bed and curl around the furry warmth in an attempt to comfort myself, the crazy woman talking to a cat. "You haven't seen what happens, you beautiful ball of fur. It isn't pretty. In fact, it is downright frightening."

Angel's wet nose sniffs at my chin, tickling me enough to make me giggle through my despair. "What have I done to be lucky enough to have you in this dreary place?"

Her only response is to snuggle closer. I continue to stroke her soft black fur that blends in perfectly with my black blankets. Comfort radiates out from her, along with heat from the little furnace within her. Taking a deep breath, I bury my face in her hair. Angel doesn't care, allowing me to take the comfort I need from her. Even in a cat, true friendship exists.

Another curiosity takes over my swirling thoughts. Who is Edgar? I can't help but be drawn to the handsome man with entrancing eyes, but something just doesn't seem right. What does he do all day? His answer to my question was not very satisfactory. What is his connection to Master

Radcliffe? There is definitely something between those two. Are they relatives?

"Why am I even bothering asking these questions? Answers seem to not come easy around here. You seem to like Edgar."

My only answer is a soft mew sound. If Angel likes him, he's got to be a good person, right? Isn't that what they always say about animals? I wonder how she would react around Master Radcliffe. It is clear she hates Gertrude-not that I blame her-but I've never seen her around Isaac or my employer.

With yet another sigh, I roll over to grab the bottle again, Angel watching with sleepy eyes. After popping two pills in my mouth, I swallow, remembering Ava's horror that I take pills without water with a low chuckle. I'm just used to taking pills. Practice makes perfect, and water isn't always available.

Placing the bottle of dreaded medicine on the night-stand, I check the time and put my phone on top of the two books I keep on the stand beneath the light. Darkness engulfs the room as I switch off the inadequate lamp and roll back over to cradle Angel again. Her soft face bumps my hand until her head rests under it. I lay in the darkness for a time, thoughts still churning, but the pills eventually drag me into a deep, dreamless slumber.

MY ALARM SOUNDS, breaking me from one of the few restful nights of sleep I have had in a long time. The stiffness works its way from my muscles with a very pleasant stretch while my eyes remain shut. Tension eases, and my joints pop. I take the time to relish a peaceful waking. It is nice to wake up to my alarm instead of my nightmares for once.

After I thoroughly enjoy my wakeup, I open my eyes, only to be startled by a pair of golden eyes glowing in the darkness that is only otherwise broken by the glow of my phone. "Angel," I breathe out slowly.

Not wanting to actually look, my hands fumble around on the stand beside my bed in search of my phone. Rattles echo in the near darkness as the bottle of sleeping pills falls from the nightstand and rolls across the floor. I whisper a quiet curse before finally finding the stack of books. When my hand runs over the top book, I'm confused. Where is my phone?

With a groan, I sit up and look around, spotting the glow of my screen coming from the top of the dresser across the room. My brows furrow. I could have sworn I placed it on top of my books. Those pills must have worked well if I forgot where I even put my phone before passing out. Shaking my head, I yawn.

My hands switch on the lamp before I drag myself out of my bed. Once I reach the dresser, I turn the alarm off and put my phone where it should be. My joints pop again as I perform another impressive stretch on my way to the closet. Grabbing the only dress not at the cleaners, I walk to the door and open it. Angel darts out and runs toward the stairs, ready to start her day.

After an uneventful shower, I clear the fog from the mirror and notice the bags under my eyes are not as pronounced. I sigh in relief. I will not rely on the pills, but I think it would be in everyone's best interest to make sure to take them when needed. It is nice to be away from the nightmares, even if only for a night. I'll take them until I feel stable again.

After drying and slipping on my dress, I grimace with displeasure and pull my wet hair into a tight bun before applying some light makeup. I stop at the kitchen to grab a blueberry bagel with cream cheese and head back to my room. I'll get to eat all of my breakfast without a cat begging for cream cheese. Who am I kidding? A little creamy goodness is worth her companionship.

Shoving another bite of bagel into my mouth, I sit on my bed and grab my phone. Surprised, I notice a text from Ava asking me how I am. I send one back, hoping it goes through. As I close it, my thumb bumps the photo icon. When the gallery opens, I chew on my lip. The first picture is not the picture I took with Ava before getting on the train. I haven't taken any other pictures since then.

I open the first photo, and my heart drops. Before me is a blue house with a beige door that I remember all too well from my nightly visits. On the steps is a ring of keys, held by a cat keychain, and a pink handbag covered in blood. A black cat sits in the window. I quickly switch to the next picture.

A man with a bloody knife runs toward the alley beside the blue house, following the trail of blood leading into the darkness. My hands shake. This can't be happening. How did these pictures get here?! Why can't I escape my nightmare?

With reluctance, I slide to the next picture, dropping my phone in horror, scrambling across the bed, and sliding over the opposite side, as if that can save me from the carnage I have just seen. The image of my bleeding body is burned into my mind, making me want to scream. I can't utter a sound as tears slide down my cheeks. That was me beside that dumpster, stabbed so many times I can't even make out the color of the dress that covered my body. How is this possible?!

I back up against the wall, not caring what my dress will look like after sliding my butt across the floor. My knees reach up to my chest before I wrap my arms around my folded legs. With my forehead on my folded knees, I sit there and shake. This can't be happening. I have to be imagining it.

Shaking, I sit like this and just breathe, trying to ignore the tingling coming on as my heart and breath lose control. I don't even try to stop the attack this time, choosing to allow myself to break down and let it happen. After an indeterminate amount of time, everything calms, and I take deep breaths to try to bring myself back to full consciousness.

It is okay. It was just your imagination. One good night of sleep won't take the crazy away. Breathe, Emma. There is no way those pictures are actually there.

I untangle my arms and legs, straightening both with protesting muscles. My shaking has calmed to slight tremors, but I still don't trust my legs. On my hands and knees, I crawl my way around the bed. My phone lies face down on the floor beside the comforter that drapes past the bottom of the bed. Stopping right beside it, I can only stare at it for a few minutes.

They are not there, Emma. You imagined it. There is no way your nightmare is on your phone. Your mind is just stuck on that dream so much that it is seeing it everywhere.

After the pep talk, I reach out my trembling hand, full of apprehension. My fingers slide over the smooth material of my phone case before wrapping around it and lifting the device from the floor. I unlock it, ready for what I don't want to see, but find my home screen lighting up my face. At first,

I can only stare at the icons covering the front. I'm not sure I can look, but I have to.

It takes my trembling thumb a couple of tries, but I manage to open my photos. Staring up at me is Ava's bright smile and the train behind us. I blink. They're not here. I really am going crazy. Will I ever truly be able to escape my dream?

CHAPTER FOURTEEN

Sharp Hangers

My hands are still shaking as I close the door. After one last apprehensive glance at my phone, I slide it into my pocket. As I exit the gloomy stairwell, I come face to face with a severe black bun. Gertrude jumps and spins around at the sound of the door. Frightened eyes convert into an angry glare.

"Has no one ever told you it isn't polite to sneak up on someone like that?!" Her dark eyes bore into me, demanding an answer.

"Sorry, madame," I say. "I didn't realize you were on the other side of the door. I'll try not to let it happen again. What's on my list today?"

Gertrude stares at me like she doesn't believe my words. "Isn't that the same dress you wore yesterday? It doesn't even look ironed."

"Yes, madame. The other ones are being cleaned."

She sighs. "Try to plan better. Master Radcliffe is not eating breakfast, so go to town and pick up your dresses. Don't come back without the master's suit as well. He is very displeased with the delay."

"Of course, madame."

"Make sure to be back by noon," she continues. "You are still on the clock, so no gallivanting around."

I fight the urge to roll my eyes. Like there is anything to do in the town anyway. "Of course, madame."

My eyes widen as my phone chimes. My supervisor's eyes narrow. "Miss Blackwood, it is severely unprofessional and rude to be playing with your phone at work!"

I shake my head, my tight bun adding momentum to the motion. "No, madame. I wasn't playing with it. I keep it on me to watch the time. I swear. I only forgot to turn the ringer off. It won't happen again."

Her hard eyes stare deep into me as I pull my phone out and switch it to silent. Gertrude huffs. "Make sure it doesn't."

Without another word, she spins and walks away briskly. I glance at my phone before sliding it back into my pocket, noticing that it was just telling me my reply to Ava didn't go through. My imagination still has me on edge, and I'm making mistakes. Gertrude doesn't need any other reasons to hate me. After growling over my stupidity, I head toward the front door.

THE BELL CHIMES as I enter the shop. The woman behind the counter looks up and offers me a shaky smile. I try to send her a warmer smile in return, unsure why she still seems so nervous. Even her voice is shaky as she asks, "Are you here for the clean garments?"

I nod. "Both mine and Master Radcliffe's please."

She moves slowly, as if pained, turning to grab the clean suit and dresses from the rack behind her. As she reaches over the counter, her sleeve slips up, causing my eyes to open wide. "What happened to your arm?"

If anything, my question seems to make her even more nervous. "O-oh it's nothing. I just snagged myself on a hanger in the back. Nothing to worry about."

Her eyes shift around, looking anywhere but at my face. Frantic, she pulls her sleeve back over her injury. I want to ask more about the fresh, deep cut on her arm, but I know she won't answer my questions. No one in this town likes to answer my questions. I'm always left in the dark, in more ways than one.

Before I can change the subject, she says, "Please tell Master Radcliffe that I sincerely apologize for the wait for his suit. I promise him it won't happen again."

"I'm sure it'll be fine. I'm sure he understands"

She looks at me as if I sprouted a couple of new heads, murmuring something I can't understand and am not sure I want to. With a sigh, I turn to walk away. As I open the door, I glance back to see her limping. A deep gash is just visible under her skirt as she walks toward the back of her shop. My mouth drops open, but I say nothing as I hurry out the door.

My slow steps down the sidewalk are interrupted by someone shouting my name. Edgar runs up to me, his piercing eyes almost making me shiver in delight. "Good morning, Edgar."

The handsome man examines me from head to toe before grimacing. "That bad?" I ask.

He shakes his head. "No. I just hate the prim and proper look. You look much better in more casual clothes. Not that you don't look good now. Wait, that came out wrong. Can I start over?"

It is hard not to laugh at the good-looking man who is usually so collected. "Sure."

"You honor me by granting my request, sweet Emma. Anyway, by the look of your attire and the agonizingly tight-looking bun, I must assume you do not have time to accompany me today." Edgar looks really pleased with himself now, having successfully overwritten his prior greeting.

"I'm still on duty, kind sir. I was only sent in to pick up some garments that were cleaned." My mind wanders back to the seamstress, making me frown.

"What's wrong?"

Eyes snapping back up to meet his, I get lost staring into those golden-brown pools. They remind me so much of Master Radcliffe's eyes, but yet, they are so different. The color is a perfect match, yet nothing that compares to the coldness seen in the depths of my employer's eyes. On the contrary, Edgar's are warm and kind. Two completely different people with the same eyes.

"Emma?"

I jump, realizing I have been staring with googly eyes instead of answering the question he asked. What did he ask again? Like he hears my thoughts, he repeats the question and elaborates. "What is wrong, Emma? You seem distracted and a bit unsettled."

Is it that clear? I guess it must be, but I've never been good at hiding my emotions. "I'm just a little disturbed and confused about my interaction with the seamstress. I'm fine, really."

"What interaction?"

He's not going to let this go, so I give in. "She was late with Master Radcliffe's order. I figured one day late wasn't a big deal, but she seemed really upset about it and told me to tell him it wouldn't happen again. She also had a cut on her arm, saying it was from hangers snagging her in back, but it looked too straight to have been that kind of accident. I saw her with one on her leg as well."

A hardness takes over those soft eyes at my words. The look in those deep depths sends shivers up my spine and makes me feel uncomfortable in front of this normally comforting presence, becoming more similar to the raspy-voiced man I try to avoid. Those eyes turn toward the manor, but they move back to my face quickly, warmth trying to suppress the unsettling coldness within. It's hard to suppress my shudder.

He licks his lips. "I apologize, Emma, but I must be going."

Edgar walks in the other direction at a quick and determined pace, not kissing my hand for the first time since the day we met. With more questions than when I started this trip to the seamstress, I walk back to the mansion overlooking the town. More questions seem to be a normal thing around here. I could write an entire book with the curiosities that plague my mind.

Isaac is at the gate, tightening some bolts, when I approach. "Ah, there you are!"

I slow down, watching him with curiosity. The handyman begins to put his tools away, finished with his job. "Gerty asked me, or rather ordered, to tell you to hang Master Radcliffe's suit on the railing at the top of the stairs. She will get it when she returns from her emergency run into town. After you take your stuff to your room, you are to report to the kitchen. There will be a list of further duties in the cleaning closet if she does not return before you finish cleaning up from lunch."

"That's quite a mouthful," I mumble.

He chuckles. "Well, Gerty has to make sure everyone knows who is in charge."

I giggle and thank him. His eyes turn solemn. "It's nice to hear that laughter on these grounds again."

My giggle falters, and I send a questioning look his way. Before I can voice the question, he turns and walks away, leaving me confused and uncertain. What can he possibly mean by that? I certainly have never giggled here before, have I? There's not much to find amusing in this creepy place, except Angel of course. Shaking my head, I walk toward the house to follow my orders.

Peter is making some sort of exotic fish for Master Radcliffe's lunch. It has been a while since I have needed to serve him, which makes me wonder how often the master of the house actually eats. The chef's jokes and banter make me smile, washing all the fear and awkwardness away for a short time. A little friendly chatter is what I need. When the clock ticks noon, he hurries from the kitchen, leaving another impressive mess behind.

I remind myself that my mother always told me that the best cooks make big messes. Peter is definitely a great cook with huge messes. With a quiet sigh, I push the cart through the door into the dining room. Master Radcliffe already waits at the end of the table. Is he humming?

Indeed, my employer is in a chipper mood today, humming and swinging his legs like a child who is very satisfied with himself. I walk past the empty plate I will need to wash, setting his meal on top of his serving dish. My boss smiles at me with a twinkle in his eyes. I'm not sure what he's humming, but it sounds familiar.

Once I'm back in my position by the door, he begins to eat. It takes me a few moments to notice when the noise of silverware on the plate stops. I look over to see him staring at me, making me shift with discomfort. Having those cold eyes on me always makes me feel like something's crawling under my skin. It's unpleasant.

"Miss Blackwood?"

"Yes, Master Radcliffe."

"Did you have a successful trip to town this morning?"

Is he engaging in conversation with me? "Yes, sir. I was told to tell you that there will be no more delays."

He laughs, a raspy and bone-chilling sound. "Good. I wouldn't expect there to be any more delays from her."

With another chuckle, he turns his attention back to the meal. There is no more conversation, and he simply gets up, grabs his hat and cane, then hobbles down the hall. Listening to the click of his cane on the hard floor, I stare in wonder. I have never seen him in this kind of mood before. He's always been stiff and unyielding, angry over every little thing. I should be happy about this change, but I find myself shivering instead.

Shaking myself out of my disturbing thoughts, I place the plates on the tray and move back to the kitchen to begin cleaning up the giant mess. Once my hands begin to prune, I glare at the perfectly clean plate I have to wash. Why do I need to wash it? Maybe I should just put it away. Washing it is a waste of time and effort.

No. I don't know how, but good ole Gerty will probably know if I don't. Instead of showing my defiance, I finish the chore before drying the dishes and placing them in their proper places. Gertrude is waiting for me outside the kitchen to tell me my only job is to organize the books in the library. She says that they are somehow all out of place.

CHAPTER FIFTEEN

Unsorting Books

With a hesitant hand, I twist the brass doorknob that leads to the library. This is not my favorite room, but it's not like any of them are. Too many hallucinations and too little space to have them in, even though this is a giant mansion inhabited by one man and his three servants. It still manages to feel over-crowded. A perplexing thought.

Shadows dance across the dark room full of books as the fire crackles in the stuffy air. A pile of books sits next to Master Radcliffe's reading chair, but everything else is in place. I slide in, eyes darting in all directions and searching for anything strange. Another fright is not something I wish to experience right now. Gertrude left a diagram showing where all the books should be organized, so I walk over to the mess left by my employer.

The first book on the pile left by Master Radcliffe deals with pain tolerance differences between different types of people. My brows furrow in thought. Why would he need to know this?

The next one deals with major arteries and how to stop patients from bleeding out. The next three books are just as bizarre, and I stop trying to figure it out. I'm not entirely sure I wish to know the answers to my increasingly numerous curiosities. I have so many questions that new ones are starting to push out old ones from my overflowing mind.

I'm also not sure where to put these books. After a little thought, I decide to put them with the medical books on the diagram since there's no demented serial killer section. The shelf is full when I reach it, so I examine it closely to see that there are so many books that don't belong there. I see fantasy, romance, action, mystery, and everything but what should be here.

This makes absolutely no sense. Master Radcliffe never puts his own books away, so the only way they get put back is by me or Gertrude. I know I put them where they belong, and Gertrude definitely would not be able to put them out of place without a hike in anxiety. How did they get out of their proper order?

Well, things do have a habit of moving when they shouldn't. No. I won't think about that. None of it happened, only hallucinations from my sleep-deprived mind. That is the only logical explanation I'll accept. If only my mind would listen to logic.

With a sigh, I begin to remove all the books in this section that don't belong. Once the stack gets knee high, I need to make a second before the first falls over. By the time I reach the end, I have four full stacks and plenty of room to add the ones my employer left out; maybe a little too much room. This is going to be an all-day task.

I check the diagram and separate the books from my piles that fit the next section, which also happens to be full. This time, I separate the books into genres as I pull them from their improper places before placing the ones from the first and moving to the next section. After what feels like hours, I have finished removing all the books that don't belong and begin placing the rest of the misplaced books where they're supposed to be.

I take a few books back to the medical section to find the

spots full and other books in their places. I know I cleaned these shelves off. How did a fantasy book get back here? With a growl, I begin my work again, only to find books misplaced over and over.

"Emma! Pay attention to what you are doing! I want to finish this today!" I growl and spin.

With a quiet scream, I jump and place my hand over my heart when I see my supervisor standing in the doorway. "Who are you talking to, Miss Blackwood?"

"No one, madame," I say, searching for words. "I just feel like I put these books in their rightful places but must have made mistakes. I keep finding more books out of place."

Gertrude sends a vicious glare around the room, searching for something I don't understand. What if they aren't hallucinations, and she knows? I shudder and shake my head to clear those irrational thoughts.

Those dark eyes land on me again. "Supper will not be served today, so try to finish it up. Once done, you may go off duty."

"Yes, madame."

After sending one last glare around the room, she leaves and closes the door behind her. It seems that her glaring at empty space has worked. I finish up without any other incident of books where they don't belong. Maybe she scared me straight, and I finally got it right. Maybe that cold stare scared something else straight. No, it was my bumbling errors that caused my overtime in the library.

No other thought is one I will accept. I really hope a few more nights of sleeping pills will help keep me from imagining these awful things I've been seeing.

I SIGH as my red hair cascades down my back in unfettered freedom. My scalp aches, so I rub my fingers over it in a gentle massage before slipping off my dress and getting ready to slide under the covers with my book. Angel is missing, but I'm sure she will show up before I go to sleep. She always does.

As I reach for my book, my phone signals I have a text message. I grab the phone and unlock the screen, hurrying to make sure I can read and reply before my spotty signal gives out. Not for the first time, I wonder if I could find a signal booster in town. I highly doubt that.

Ava: I know you don't have a decent signal there, but that isn't stopping me from worrying. I hope you get this.

After glancing at the upper right corner of my screen, I see that I do have a weak signal. My heart swells with hope. It needs to hold for a little bit.

Me: I seem to have a weak signal now, and I'm not sure how long it will last. I'm fine. Stop worrying.

As usual, when this subject comes up, I watch the three dots appear and disappear for a while. She finally figures out what she wants to say, although I'm sure it isn't her original thought. My best friend worries too much.

Ava: That's good. You're getting some sleep?
Me: Yeah.
Ava: I know this is text, but that wasn't very convincing. Are you truly?

I sigh. It seems that I can't hide anything from her, even at this distance. Hiding behind a phone screen doesn't help keep my friend from knowing what I'm feeling.

Me: I am fine, Ava. I bought some sleeping pills to make sure I get enough sleep. I am totally fine.

Ava: Sleeping pills? Do they have a doctor there you can talk to?

Me: I said I'm fine...

Ava: I know. I know you hate when I ask, but I worry after last time.

The memories make me shudder, but I can't stop them this time. Unwilling to listen to my wishes, my mind takes me back to a time I don't want to remember.

"I am fine."

Ava stares at me with worry, and I can hear my parents standing right outside the entranceway to the kitchen. Why can't anyone ever just listen to me when I tell them not to worry? I think I know myself best.

"You are not fine, Emma," Ava argues. "Please, I just want you to get help."

"Help doesn't help," I counter. "You know this. I'm not crazy, so I wish everyone would stop making me feel like I am."

My best friend chews her lip, stalling with a sip of water. "You haven't slept in weeks, Emma."

Knuckles white on my own glass of water, I glare at the only true friend I've ever had; a friend that only wants to help. "I am not seeing another shrink. All he will do is drug me up again. Do you have any idea how that feels?! I am not crazy. They are only nightmares."

Tears glisten in her bright eyes, turning her blues into shifting oceans. "Emma, please..."

The glass is halfway to my mouth, but it flies back to the table in anger. Shattering, the glass cuts into my hands and spills water everywhere. I watch the water flow across the table and drop down to the floor and onto my jeans. I'm hypnotized as I watch the clear liquid turn pink, then red.

"Emma! You're bleeding!"

I barely notice the sound of Ava pushing her chair back to run for a towel. She wraps my hand and calls for my parents, but I only watch the red running and smearing all over the table without a word. The blood is mine, just like in my nightmare.

Gasping, I come back to the here and now. That was strange. I've never had a flashback like that. Memories are one thing, but this was more than that. It's like I was reliving it. I close my eyes and will the tears away. It takes a lot of effort, but I remind myself she is my best friend and only wants to help. I'm tired, and that's why my anger is getting the better of me. I know the signs. I can stop it this time. I know I can.

Me: I know you do. I'm sorry for being short with you. Please, don't tell my parents. I promise to find someone, even if I have to do phone sessions if I get out of hand. I promise you.

Ava doesn't respond right away, and I fear I have lost her again, but the signal is still there. I lay my head back and hope she doesn't go running to my parents. They won't understand either. My phone pings again.

Ava: I trust you. I swear I do. I don't mean to be a pain. I love you like the sister I never had. You're a much better sibling than my brothers.

I laugh. She always exaggerates. My friend is very close to her older brothers, but I agree that we are more like sisters than friends.

Me: I love you too. I swear I won't put you through that again. I will make time to see you again soon. Maybe we can meet halfway sometime.

Message failed.

I growl in frustration as the bars disappear from my phone and throw it across the bed. Ava will understand. She knows my signal is dismal here. Using the payphone is now at the top of my list. I need to hear her voice again.

My head lands against the headboard behind me. "I feel so alone," I whisper.

As soon as those words leave my mouth, I feel a weight land on my bed and jump. Golden eyes look up at me, and I pull the black cat into my arms. She doesn't protest, only purrs and rubs her head against my chin in greeting.

I reach over and grab my bottle of pills, downing one before snuggling down into bed with the purring ball of black fur. I will take these pills as long as they help and look for further mediation as needed. I will fulfill my promise to my best friend. The dim light disappears as I switch it off, and Angel snuggles closer. I run my hand over her soft fur.

"At least I have you."

CHAPTER SIXTEEN

Interventions

The alarm wakes me from another dreamless sleep. Grateful for the rest, I stretch with a huge smile, disturbing a certain black cat from her own slumber. Angel bares her sharp teeth with a huge yawn before stretching her front legs, then each of her back legs.

After receiving a loud purr for my scratch, I reach over and grab my blaring phone. I avoid looking too much at the screen and turn the alarm off. As I put the phone back, I realize that something is missing. My bottle of pills was sitting right beside the light that I switch on. It's not there now.

Sitting up, I move the books around to see if it fell between something, but it is nowhere to be seen. Looking down, I find the little white pills scattered all over the floor, the empty bottle by the door, and the cap nowhere to be seen. I scramble from the bed, landing on my hands and knees. With a wince, I reach under my knee and remove the pill embedded in it from my landing. One by one, the pills go back into their bottle, and I find the cap in the dreadful corner. How in the world did that happen?

When I return the pills to the stand, I make sure to tightly wedge them in between the books and lamp to keep them in place. I'm sure they were squarely on the stand with the cap tight. Maybe Angel knocked them off, and maybe the cap wasn't as tight as I thought it was. How else did they end up all over the floor?

Oh well. I'm sure the floor is clean enough to eat off of thanks to Gertrude's diligence. Angel hisses as I open the door, needing a sprint to the bathroom to relieve my exploding bladder. I almost get instant relief when a black bun hovering over an emotionless face nearly gives me a heart attack.

Angel growls and runs between my supervisor's legs, making her stumble and yell, "Stupid fleabag! Can't you just stay gone?!"

I bite back a retort that would probably end with me jobless. "Madame, I'm not late am I?"

Gertrude stops scolding my only friend in this mansion and turns back to me. It is taking everything I have not to bounce up and down to try to avoid losing my teetering control. I'm sure she wouldn't appreciate a new puddle at her feet. I hope she hurries.

Dark eyes blink at me. "No, Miss Blackwood. I wanted to get to you before you started your morning routine. The master is out for the day. Your duty is to clean the rooms in this hall. There is no cleaning closet up here, but I am sure you can manage to get a cart up."

The black bun retreats down the hall, and I sigh. As she disappears into the staircase door, I remember my distress and run to the bathroom as quickly as possible.

WITH MY WET hair pulled into a tight bun, I survey myself in the bathroom mirror. I really don't think black is my color, but everything else about me is looking much better. The bags under my eyes are almost gone already, and the color has returned to my cheeks. It is simply amazing just how much two nights of uninterrupted sleep can do.

I can only hope it lasts. Chewing my bottom lip, I can't stop thinking about what happens when my dreams break through the drug haze. When I can no longer block them, I slowly slip into a fog. Not wanting to remember more, I shake my head and sigh.

I walk into the kitchen, opening the fridge to see what is here to eat. A parcel wrapped in foil meets my eyes. It is labeled as breakfast with heating instructions. Peter is such a keeper. His wife is one very lucky woman. I begin to wonder if Edgar can cook, but something tells me he isn't used to cooking for himself. Why am I even thinking of him like that? I barely even get to see him, and that thought makes me sad.

I unwrap my food to find a ham and cheese omelet within the foil. After reheating it, I sit at the table and dig in, letting the flavors burst on my tongue in pleasure. Halfway through, I drop a piece on my lap. When I see the spot form on my dress, my initial thought is panic, but I remember I am cleaning today. My apron will cover the dark stain from Gertrude's judgemental gaze. It should be easy to clean. I mean, if she can get that red stuff out of my employer's shirt, surely she can get a little breakfast matter out too. I shudder and remind myself not to think of what I saw on that suit.

After cleaning my plate, I head down to the cleaning closet. Once the cart is at the bottom of the stairs, I groan at the task before me. One step at a time, I drag the heavy cart up the staircase, banging it against the step with each move upward. I almost lose it a few times, but I am able to catch it before it tumbles and spills, then continuing to drag the load upward.

I stumble into the hallway, pulling the cart with my sweaty hands. Stumbling, I sit on the dark carpet lining the hallway floor and pant until my breathing slows. After wiping the sweat from my forehead with my apron, I make my way to the kitchen for a drink of water and to check my phone. With a sigh, I realize it took way too long to get the stupid cart up the stairs. You'd think Gertrude would devise a better system for cleaning the servant's wing.

After a little thinking, I decide to start with the bathroom at the other end of the dark hall. This way, I can already have the cart close to the stairs when I am finished. The wheels half over the threshold to the bathroom, I begin my chore.

My face blurs as the glass cleaner covers the mirror and begins to run, reminding me of the crack and river of red I saw days ago. Shivers run over my spine, but I tell myself it was only a hallucination from my sleep-deprived mind. The blood was gone when I told Gertrude about it. It was only my sanity slipping after severe lack of sleep. I need to get a hold of my mental state.

Squeaks echo in the windowless bathroom as I wipe the dry cloth over the dripping mirror. To make sure I get every speck of dirt, I use my nails to squeeze the cloth into the crack along the frame of the mirror. Every speck of dirt must be eradicated, or I risk a mark on my permanent record. At the bottom, I see something spot the cloth, so I run it over again, trying to dislodge whatever dirt is in that tiny crevice. It's stubborn, so I scrub hard enough that my fingers ache.

After I pull the cloth away, I see a line of blood on it and cry out. Dropping the cloth, I stumble backward, trip over the cleaner I left on the floor, and land on the hard tile butt first. I moan as pain radiates up my tailbone and into my back. Reaching over, I grab the cloth. The blood is still there, stubbornly refusing to listen to my pleas that I'm imagining it again.

It isn't fresh blood, almost like it is left over from the incident that never happened. I roll the cloth into a tight ball and toss it toward the cart blocking the door, sliding back until I'm propped up in the corner. I look down at my shaking hands, but before I can process what is happening, another past vision takes over stronger than any flashback could.

"Emma, please listen to us. We know you aren't crazy; you just need some help."

I try to ignore the rationality of my dad's words as I stare at the shaking hands in my lap. Clenching my hands into fists does nothing to stop their insistent shaking. Nothing works anymore. I can't remember the last time I slept more than a few minutes at a time. The pills don't work anymore.

My nightmare has begun to manifest in my awake hours, making me see things that I used to only see while I sleep. None of it makes sense anymore, but I'm not crazy. I don't need to talk to someone who will make me feel like I am. I only want to feel normal.

"I will be fine, Dad," I mumble, unable to take my eyes off my trembling hands.

Mom kneels in front of me, but I refuse to meet her gaze. "We just worry about you. We are afraid of what not sleeping will do to you. I know you won't admit it, but we know you are starting to see things. Let us help you. Please."

Her soft hands encompass my own, and tears threaten to escape my burning eyes. This is the woman who gave birth to me, loved me through all my tantrums and attitude-filled years. How can I say no to her?

They'll only be forced to pay for a doctor that can't help, yet again. I shake my head, pulling my hands from hers as I stand.

"I'm eighteen. I can make this decision on my own. I will be fine. Another doctor will not be able to help me. It will blow over eventually."

If I look at them, I know I will crumble, so I walk away without looking up. They continue to plead with me, but I walk toward the front door without listening to their concerned words. No one can help me. Why should I put my parents through all the doctors' payments when the doctors never help?

"They're just dreams," they always tell me. I've been drugged by every medication known to man, talked to until my ears felt like they would bleed, and even hypnotized. None of it has worked. Nothing will. This is my reality, and I have to learn to live with it. They're just dreams, but what happens when the dreams become real?

Tears drip from my chin as I stare at the tile under me, my hands shaking uncontrollably. Why am I having these visions of the past now? I haven't reached that point yet, so why am I seeing this already? I've been sleeping, so reality shouldn't be blurring.

Is it my own fear of what is to come? Should I just go home and accept help that never works? It doesn't seem worth it to pay so much money for doctors that can't help me. Mom and dad will help, but I can't keep doing that to them; it's too much of a burden. They deserve so much more.

My head falls into my hands as the tears flow harder. I curl up in the corner and sob until I am able to will the memories away. Still sniffling, I drag myself to my feet and walk over to put the cloth in my dirty linen bag without looking at it.

I grab a bucket and pour some cleaner into it before placing it in the tub to fill with bubbly water. As the water thunders into the empty bucket, I turn around to grab a mop. I close my eyes tight, fighting the tears that still try to come. The mop is placed against the wall, and I walk back for the bucket. I scream.

The bucket is not full of water. Instead, the thick and sticky crimson liquid spills over the top and begins to cover the bottom of the tub in a swirling froth. Small ivory pieces start to float to the top of the bucket like bubbles rising. Against all reason, I bend down to look closer. Another scream erupts from me as I realize human teeth are floating within the bucket of blood, some cracked beyond repair.

My hands fly up from the side of the tub I lean on, bumping the bucket and splashing blood everywhere. The tub is half full when I stumble and fall again. Some of the red liquid has splashed out, spotting my dress and arms. As I scramble back, the showerhead turns on, spewing more blood.

I try to stand and run, but my feet slip on the blood my dress has smeared over the floor. I curl into a ball and will it to go away. This can't be real.

CHAPTER SEVENTEEN

Twisted Fork

My breathing is shallow as I refuse to look toward the tub. Surely the blood is overflowing by now, reaching for me, but I'm tired of these visions. I can't look. My eyes squeeze shut even harder. What if it is real this time?

When I decide I've been laying on the floor long enough, I uncurl from my fetal position and find nothing wet on the tile beneath me. I look down, noticing the blood is no longer coating my arms or dress. I cautiously lift my head up to look in the direction of the tub, fearful of what I might see.

The showerhead no longer spews crimson liquid. My legs wobble as I push myself to my feet, unable to control my shaking body. After a particularly rough wobble, I fall back to my knees and crawl the rest of the way. My knuckles turn white as I place my hands on the side of the ceramic basin. With a few deep breaths, I pull myself up enough to look into the tub.

The bucket lies on its side, suds and water circling toward the drain as the water still gushes from the faucet. I stare in wonder and keep telling myself I am going crazy. It is getting worse, and I don't understand why. I've been sleeping the last couple of nights, so the visions should be easing up at the very least.

Shaky hands place the bucket upright, and it fills

quickly. Enough soap is left to bubble up to the top of my black bucket, so I don't need to use more. Once full, I turn the water off and slide back to the floor, covering my eyes with my hands.

My breathing is unsteady as I sigh into my palms, my hot breath blowing back into my face. I have to get back to work. Why is it getting so hard to concentrate lately? Why are the visions still coming?

With a sigh, I stand and lift the full bucket with a grunt. The mop slides across the floor until the entire bathroom is spotless. I set the bucket outside in the hall, waiting for the floor to dry before emptying it. As I wait, I lean against the cool wall and rub my eyes. When will life be normal again? Has my life ever truly been normal?

"Miss Blackwood!"

Both elbows slam into the wall as I stand up straight. Unwilling to voice my discomfort, I cross my arms to rub my elbows. "Yes, Madame?"

"Are you lounging on the job?"

"No, Madame. I was just taking a quick breath after finishing the bathroom."

"How much have you gotten done so far?"

"Um," I say, reluctant to tell her I have only cleaned the bathroom. I'm sure that this will upset her.

"I will take that to mean you have only completed the bathroom." My supervisor glares at me, and I wither under her gaze. "I don't see why Master Radcliffe keeps you. You are so lazy."

"No, Madame! It took me a long time to get the cart up the stairs, then the bucket spilled while I was filling it to mop."

Yes, let's go with that. She doesn't need to know any

more than that. My employer isn't required to know of the visions that have been plaguing me. She doesn't need to be told that the tub filled with imaginary blood while I huddled in the corner crying.

Gertrude huffs. "You will need to finish tomorrow, and you will finish it all before quitting time. You may leave the cart. Master Radcliffe made a mess in the sitting room, but I need to head into town again. You are to clean that room. With your speed, that is probably all you'll be able to finish today anyway."

I bite my tongue to keep it from getting me into further trouble. "I promise to have it done, Madame."

Gertrude's eyes narrow, but she turns and walks away, bun bobbing behind her. With a sigh, I realize the room is mostly dry and dump the slightly dirty water down the drain, then tip the bucket upside down to dry in the bathtub. I rub my still-aching elbows and head down the stairs. At least I don't need to drag the cart down just yet.

I enter the sitting room. Three large dark blue couches circle yet another fireplace, a black carpet covering the wooden floor between them. My eyes widen at the mess, and I run to the cleaning closet to grab another cart. This is one time Gertrude's neurotic need for cleanliness is helpful, plenty of cleaning supplies.

The first thing I do is sweep up the pile of ash that is spilling from the brick fireplace. Next, the figures atop the mantle are straightened and positioned. After that, I begin picking up the books scattered all over the floor, only to find a glass of bourbon soaked into the carpet. The books are slightly damp, and I'm unsure how to fix this.

I clean the covers off as well as I can and fan them out on top of the cart in hopes they will dry well enough. Turning back to this catastrophe of a room, I see couch cushions all out of place, the ashtray laying on the wet carpet, and the carpet crumpled in a couple of places. I place my hands on my hips. How does one grown man make such a mess?

Laughing, I realize I'm standing the same way Ava does when she scolds me. With that thought, I can picture Ava with her hands on her hips, staring at me from across the room. Before I can register more than amusement, I find that I'm no longer in the sitting room of a mansion in Restless Hills.

Ava stands and stares at me with her hands on her narrow hips. Mom and Dad laugh behind me, and I join in for the first time in weeks. My parents love Ava, and I can't blame them at all. We all stand in the kitchen, cleaning up after a family supper.

It feels good to laugh again. Life has been so heavy lately, and nights don't offer a reprieve. There isn't much rest when you can't sleep. Of course, this moment can't last.

Ava's form begins to waver in my vision. Instead of my best friend, a man with a knife and covered in shadows stands where she once stood. All I can see on his face is that smirk that always precedes the pain. I can hear my name being called from a distance, but the only thing I can focus on is that smirk and the gleam of the weak light on the knife in his hands.

He's here to kill me again, but I won't go easy this time. For some reason, there is a fork on the railing of my house steps this time. I grab it, then launch myself at my attacker. He moves at the last second, but the fork sinks into his shoulder, causing him to cry out. Triumph overwhelms me, but I'm pulled away with strong arms.

That's when I realize I'm no longer outside the house. My dad keeps my struggling body still in our kitchen once again. Mom sits on the floor next to Ava, pressing a towel against her shoulder, a bloody fork laying on the floor next to them.

Oh no!

I pull my hand from my open mouth, unable to stop the tears the memory evokes. I cry at all the pain I have put my best friend through. Ava has been through so much for me, and I can't understand why she puts up with it. How can she still love me as her best friend after everything that has happened? Why didn't I listen to her?

With a shuddering sigh, I get to work straightening up the room, my thoughts a whirlwind of regret and longing. Why are the pills not working? I know the last time my dreams overwhelmed me, they helped for a little while before my nightmare broke through. Why am I still having these visions and memories?

Once the room is as clean as possible, I return my cart, take the books back to the library, and turn toward the kitchen. It's almost five o'clock, so supper should be ready soon. I run into Gertrude on the way, but she tells me he's not eating in the dining room. I can return to the servant's wing. The garlic pork chops I find in the servant's fridge barely have any flavor as I eat my premade supper. I'm not even hungry, but I know I need to eat, so I continue to cut the pork and move it to my mouth.

With a heavy sigh, I rinse my plate but decide to completely wash it in the morning. When I enter my room, the picture of Ava and I catches my attention. I walk over to the dresser and lift the picture frame in my hands. My fingers gently caress my friend's face. I miss her.

After sitting on my bed, I grab my phone and flip through the pictures. I find the one of Ava during our trip to the beach last year. Zooming in, I focus on the scar left on her shoulder from the fork I plunged into her when I believed she was the man from my nightmare.

"I'm so sorry, Ava," I whisper.

She forgave me instantly, but I don't think I have ever truly forgiven myself. Ava is my best friend. We've known each other since we were babies. How could I do that to her? How could she forgive me so easily?

She always forgives me. I don't deserve such a wonderful friend. What have I ever given her but grief and worry? I open my text messages and select our conversation. My thumbs tremble, resolve wavering. No, I need to.

Me: Ava... What do you see in me? All I've ever given you is mental, emotional, and physical pain. Why do you still love me like a sister? I don't deserve your love. I don't deserve you. I am so sorry for everything I have done to you. I wish I could take it all back.

I stare at the message for a couple minutes, then press the send button, wanting to say so much more but unable to put it into text. With the signal I have, I doubt this will go through, but I need to try. My friend needs to know I'm sorry.

My phone thumps on the nightstand, and I reach for my pills. They aren't there. Frantic, needing another night of undisturbed sleep, I throw the books on the floor. When the bottle is nowhere to be found, I get down on my hands and knees to look under my nightstand. They aren't here.

Lifting the comforter, I look under the bed and scream at the eyes looking back. My head bounces off the leg of the stand by my bed, but I still manage to throw myself backward, eyes not leaving the bottom of the bed. A furry black face pops out from beneath the comforter, meowing at me in question.

A sigh of relief escapes me, and I grab my phone for its flashlight. The pills are not under my bed or the dresser. I even check the closet. With one last burst of hope, I check the pockets of my apron without success.

Tears sting my eyes as I sit on top of my bed. I need those pills. I can't deal with the nightmare, not tonight. Curling into a ball on top of all my blankets, I cry while ignoring the cat trying to comfort me. Despair consumes me.

CHAPTER EIGHTEEN

Lost in Dreams

Sweat drips from my forehead as I jerk awake, startling the black cat who is snoring beside me. My nightmare has come back, and it felt much more intense this time, as if punishing me for trying to find peace. This is not a good sign. I know what comes next. I need to try to find help to forestall further slipping. A weak hope that this town has some sort of doctor I can speak to enters my mind. I promised Ava I would seek help if needed, and it's needed now.

Slowly sitting up, I groan from the cold stiffness that happens when someone sleeps on top of their covers in an apron and uncomfortable dress. It takes everything I have to swing my legs over the side of the bed and pick up my phone after switching on the light.

With a sigh, I realize I don't need to be up for another four hours, but there's absolutely no way I can go back to sleep now. That's when I notice I have a text message. Opening it, I remember the message I had sent my best friend before falling asleep. I rub my eyes and read her response.

Ava: Is everything ok? I will always be there for you, and you know that. That was a rough point in your life. What kind of friend would I be if I abandoned you during it? I love you like a sister, and you deserve that love 100 times over. What's going on? CALL ME!!!!

I blink the threatening tears from my eyes and take a deep breath. There's no signal, of course, so I decide to wait to reply. I can eat breakfast, but I'm not hungry. Instead of eating another flavorful meal I can't taste, I get up and take my shower.

Once I'm dressed with my hair in the required brain-sucking bun, I grab my cleaning cart to get to work. There's still time before I'm required to start my shift, but I need to keep busy. Working will help keep me out of my head for a while, which is what I truly need. Won't Gertrude be surprised?

Each room is as dreary as mine. Dark rugs, dark wood walls and floor, and dark blankets make for a very dreary day in dimly lit rooms. It's not like this darkness is any different than the rest of the house, and it fits my mood perfectly. My day seems as normal as a day in this place can be.

That is until I reach my last bedroom. I dust the dresser and nightstand before starting on the bedding. After removing the comforter and placing it in the dirty linen bag, I remove the top sheet. I stare in horror at the sight before me. The fitted sheet is no longer made of dark fabric and is stained with brown blood. Something about the patterns tickles another locked memory in the back of my mind.

With a scream, I sit up, clutching my pajama shirt. I'm drenched with sweat, my heart is racing, and my breath is coming fast. That was the first time in weeks I have slept more than a few minutes at a time, and it has not gone well.

Looking down, I swear I can still see the stab wounds all over my upper body. With shrill screams barreling from my chest, I tear at my shirt, then dig at the wounds covering me with my fingernails. Why won't they disappear? Make them go away!

"Emma!"

How did my mom get here? She's never in my nightmare.

"Emma, stop! You're hurting yourself!"

That's Dad's voice, but the man who grabs me is covered in shadows with my blood on his hands. I scream, punching and twisting to get free. The hands leave my shoulders, and my fingers go back to my knife wounds, nails raking across skin. I'm leaving deep gashes through my torn shirt, but they are nowhere as deep as the holes made by the knife.

"Emma! No!"

I scream and struggle, trying to twist from my murderer's grasp. Footsteps echo in the distance, but those hands won't leave me. It is hard to tell how long I struggle, but multiple sets of hands begin reaching for me. I scream and try to roll away.

A prick on my neck frightens me further, but I won't stop fighting. A few moments later, I can no longer fight. I'm carried from my bed and placed on a table with wheels. Who knows where this evil man is taking me? The last thing I see as darkness takes me is the pattern of bloodstains all over my sheets.

Stains that I see now; stains on sheets that shouldn't have blood spattered on them. I close my eyes and breathe hard, hands pulling the red hair from my tight bun. My body begins to shake uncontrollably. When I open my eyes, the sheets are no longer covered in blood, their normal clean darkness stares back at me. I laugh at the insanity I am now lost in.

I don't realize my feet are moving until my back hits a corner, and I slide slowly down it until my arms are hugging my knees to my chest. Memories flash before me, completely out of my control as I begin to sob. I'm truly going crazy again. I don't even bother to stop the panic attack that takes over me.

THE ICE-COLD WATER cascades down my throat, further grounding me after my experience. I lean on the counter, head hanging low as I contemplate everything. Will I ever escape the never-ending cycle I'm stuck in? It seems very unlikely.

No matter how much I fight, I always slip back into my temporary madness. Maybe I should have stayed home. I doubt this tiny town will have the help I need. The next town over might, but who can I ask? I don't want to risk my job. Only Edgar feels safe as a confidant, but I am not ready to bare my crazy to him. There's no one else.

Tears sting my eyes. After a few quick sobs and sniffles, I stand straight and take a deep breath to calm myself. Opening the fridge, I stare at the food that holds no interest. It's lunchtime, and the fridge is full of all kinds of delectables from Peter, but it all looks bland and disgusting.

I may have closed the door a little louder than I need to when I hear the bottles in the door clink together, but my frustration doesn't care. I'm just not hungry, and there is no point in eating, even if it is lunchtime. With a sigh, I take another drink and head back to the hallway, tucking the loose strands of my hair back in the bun.

Staring between the cart and the stairs, I grimace. I'd love to just leave this up here, but I know old Gerty would have a fit. So, one step at a time, I maneuver the heavy cart down what feels like way too many stairs to fit in the mansion.

At the bottom of the stairwell, I stare at the door, afraid to try to balance the cart on the last step with only one hand. Maybe I should request an elevator be put in. This place is big and empty enough to fit one. I laugh at the thought of asking Gertrude where the suggestion box is.

Careful not to be squished by a heavy cart, I release one hand from it and reach for the handle on the door. After getting it open, I stare between the door and the cart with a groan. Using my foot to brace the heavy chunk of dark wood, I twist to grab the cart handle with both hands and pull it down the last step.

With relief, I pull the cart through the door, sighing after avoiding spilling everything on the floor. When I am almost through, the door slams shut, cart stuck in it. A less-than-graceful pull dislodges my burden, and I fly backward. My eyes widen when I hit something softer than the floor or wall and hear an undignified, "Miss Blackwood!"

I yelp, barely catching my fall, and spin to find my supervisor with the usual unhappy disappointment on her face that is always present when she looks at me. "Miss Blackwood, what do you think you are doing?! You could have injured me."

"I'm sorry, Madame," I reply, breathless from my exercise and fright. "The cart got stuck."

"And your solution was to yank it out instead of finding some way to prop the door open? Any damages will be taken from your pay, Miss Blackwood."

I chew my lip. "I didn't mean to, Madame. I didn't sleep well and couldn't think of another solution right then."

She huffs. "So you're done?"

Why does she seem surprised? "With upstairs, yes."

"Very well. Take the dirty linens you collected to the laundry room and wash them, then stack them on the shelves in the linen closet."

"Yes, Madame." She's already halfway down the hall.

This is really not turning out to be my day, or many days. How else can I screw up? Better not ask that question, or it might be taken as a challenge. I wonder how long my list of errors is in my record. Record... I'm not a child. Angry, I stuff the cart in the closet and grab the dirty linen bags off it. Time to go wash the mostly clean comforters and sheets.

THE CLUNKING of the dryer is accentuated by the whirring of the washer. I feel like I'm tumbling around, just like the linens in the dryer. I'm just going around and around, but unlike the dryer, I do not see an end to my cycle.

Life is good for a while, only disturbed by the nightmare every once in a while. That dream begins to appear more often, eventually keeping me from sleep for too long. I fight the encroaching madness but am never able to stop it forever. When control is lost, I'm sucked into a world of doctors, needles, and pills.

The buzzer sounds, breaking me from my dark thoughts. I pull the dry linens out and transfer the wet ones to the dryer before throwing another load in to be cleansed. That's what the doctors try to do. They try to cleanse the insanity out of me. My hands tuck and fold the still-warm sheets into an organized square. These sheets will be placed on beds during the next wash, only to start the whole cycle of clean to dirty to clean again.

Am I no different from the soiled sheets? Will I ever be left alone? Will I forever be pulled through this vicious cycle? Will I never be free?

CHAPTER NINETEEN

Crumbs Under the Table

With a sigh, I roll over. Angel has long since stopped tolerating my constant movement and hopped over to the dresser across from me. Her golden eyes glow in the soft light, closing sleepily and reopening with every one of my movements. Something feels right about this feline watching over me, something familiar.

I reach over and grab my phone. It's after one, but I have no interest in sleeping. I know I should, or I'll risk falling deeper into the familiar darkness. Logic no longer appeals to me. All I want to do is avoid being murdered again.

With a groan that is a mixture of frustration and exhaustion, I lift myself to a sitting position and stand. The hallway is darker than usual as I make my way to the kitchen. The glow of the refrigerator illuminates the dark room. I grab some sliced cheddar and take a box of crackers from the cupboard next to the refrigerator. The fridge door shuts, enveloping the kitchen in darkness again.

After turning on the low light, I sit down for my snack. Crumbs cascade to the table, and probably the floor, as I take my first bite. I know I will need to clean up the mess, but at least it will give me something to occupy the long night with.

The cracker and cheese fall from my hands at the sound of a floorboard creaking out in the hallway. All sounds stop, including my breathing, and I strain to listen for any other sound. There it is again, closer.

I cover my mouth with my hand and slip to the floor. My earlier assumption is proved to be right as crumbs stick to the other palm while I crawl under the table on the cold kitchen floor. Arms around my knees, I hope whatever it is passes me over and wish the short tablecloth held better protection from sight.

My heart thunders in my ears, and I'm sure it can be heard all through the house. Another floorboard squeaks, this one right outside the kitchen doorway. I press my teeth into my lower lip to stop its trembling, clamping my hand harder over my mouth and willing my heart to stop echoing. My lungs burn for air, but I refuse to breathe.

A foot ambles into view, shuffling with a strange limp. As it gets closer, I see the other and notice the naked legs attached to them. Dirt clings to the obviously female legs and under the toenails. Before my eyes, I see a river of blood flow over each leg.

I can feel my entire body shake and try to gauge the success I might find at making a dash for the door. She is now beside the table, so my chances are better than they were before. Those thoughts stop with the feet. The table above me shifts as weight is applied to it, and I feel paralyzed.

Blood drips onto the floor, pattering as each drop splatters onto the mostly clean surface next to me. I want to scream. I want to cry. I can do neither of these things.

As the feet and legs shift, a hand dangles down, blood dripping from missing fingertips. Red hair, sticky with darker red, dangles down below the edge of the tablecloth. The hair reminds me of the woman I saw in the bathroom, bleeding unnatural amounts of blood from her throat. That thought makes my trembling stop, further paralyzing me into a crippling fear.

A face comes into view, and I can no longer hold back my tears and screams. She stares at me, one blue eye hanging loose from its socket and dangling against her bloody cheek. I scream louder, jumping up and slamming my head off the bottom of the table.

Cheese and crackers rain down around me, but I ignore them. Pain radiates from the top of my head, and I try to pull away when I see one fingerless hand reach for me. Her blood drips onto my bare feet, warm as it slides between my naked toes. As I close my eyes, I feel strong hands grab my shoulders.

I turn and swing, my fist meeting with something hard and sending a howl of pain from my attacker's mouth. When I realize that sounds too deep to be a woman, I open my eyes and see Isaac rubbing his calf. Frantic, I search the area, finding no trace of the bloody woman with hair like mine.

After filling my struggling lungs with air, I scramble from beneath the table. Isaac steps back warily, looking confused and startled. "Emma? I couldn't sleep and decided to fix the stairwell light Gerty has been nagging me about. I heard you screaming."

I scramble to my feet but stumble, and Isaac helps me into a chair. My eyes continue to dart around, and my breaths come out in panicked sobs. "Did you see her?"

An unknown look flashes in the handyman's eyes. "Who?"

Something in his voice tells me he isn't being truthful, like he knows who I saw. Before I can question him further, he slides into the chair across from me and runs his greasy hand through his hair.

"There was a woman with red hair just here. She was covered in blood and...."

...missing an eye.

Yes, Emma. Let's let Isaac know you are going crazy too. Why am I willing to talk to him after hiding it from everyone else? I shake my head. I can't be stupid. "Never mind. I think I may have just fallen asleep."

A hideously nervous laugh escapes me, and I can tell he is not convinced. "If that was a dream, those are some pretty disturbing images."

"You have no idea," I breathe, then clear my throat. "I'm sorry to have worried you, but I'm fine. My active imagination tends to act up when I'm tired."

He cocks his head to the side, examining me closely. "Why are you awake at this hour?"

"Same as you," I counter. "I couldn't sleep and thought a snack would be helpful."

The groundskeeper chuckles. "Well, it must have worked if you fell asleep at the table and dreamed about bloody women."

My fake smile falls. "If you don't mind me asking, what happened to the girls before me?"

Isaac scratches his neck and looks away. "They didn't work out."

"Why not?"

"They weren't the right fit."

I can tell my questioning is making him uncomfortable, but I don't relent. "So, they went home?"

"They left here. I cannot tell you where they went from there." His tone makes me suspicious, but he stands before I can ask more questions. Afraid to be alone, I beg him to sit again. With extreme reluctance, he slides back into his chair.

Angel picks that moment to enter the kitchen, whiskers twitching as she sniffs the air. Isaac watches her. With a disinterested glance at Isaac, those golden eyes land on the cheese on the floor. This is the first time I have ever seen her indifferent to anyone. She seems to be attached to me, likes Edgar, and hates Gertrude.

Isaac elicits no reaction from the black cat whatsoever. I find this strange.

"She seems to take to you." I jump at Isaac's voice. He raises a blond eyebrow, but I laugh my reaction off.

"She's my roomie."

He nods but looks between me and the cat, eyes twinkling in surprise and deep thought. "Interesting," he murmurs.

"What is?"

My coworker clears his throat. "Now that your roomie is here, I'm going to get back to bed. The light is fixed, so Gerty can stop nagging me."

He is out the door before I can protest. Leaving the cheese for Angel, I clean up the mess on the table and head back to my room. I climb into bed with my back against the headboard and grab my book. The door is closed, but Angel seems to always find her way back in.

MY STOMACH RUMBLES as I close the last page of my book. I'll need to get a new one today. I ignore my growling stomach and stretch. Looking at my phone, I realize I have plenty of time to exchange it for a new one before my shift starts.

The black cat on my lap acts insulted when I move and stand, but she curls up on my pillow and goes back to sleep.

I envy cats and their ability to remain alert and asleep at the same time, as well as their ability to sleep the day away. I've gotten no sleep at all. Do cats dream?

When I pass the kitchen, I don't even look in. Before I start my day, I'll need to make sure Angel finished cleaning up my mess to avoid having the messy kitchen put on my record, but as of now, I couldn't care less. The cool stairs chill my naked feet, and I wish I would have put socks on. When I reach the door, I slowly open it but stop when it's barely cracked. I hear voices.

"What do you mean they're showing themselves to her?" That's Gertrude's voice. Does she mean me?

Isaac answers. "What do you think I mean, Gerty?"

"I have told you thousands of times to not call me that!"

Isaac sighs. "And I have heard you each time, but I don't tolerate your bullying."

My eyes widen. Sure, I have heard Isaac tease Gertrude, but I never heard him talk to her with such derision.

"You are a nuisance," Gertrude hisses. "Why do I have to be stuck with you?"

"Because I am good at what I do."

My supervisor growls. "You are exasperating, but stop distracting me. They have never shown themselves to the girls before."

"Maybe Emma is different."

Gertrude laughs. "Miss Blackwood? She may be a mediocre servant, and I say that generously, but there isn't anything special about the girl."

My brows furrow. That was uncalled for.

"Well, you tell me why they are revealing themselves to her."

Wait. Are they talking about the dead girls, the strange things happening, or both?

Gerty sighs. "I don't know. She does seem to be in fright a lot. I've tried to calm them, but at this point, not even Master Radcliffe can do anything about it."

They know?! Gertrude has been looking at me like I'm crazy! My mind goes back to previous encounters, and I remember the cold stares she would give to empty spaces. My blood runs cold. Swallowing the lump in my throat, I softly close the door and all but run up the stairs. This cannot be happening. The strange things aren't real. I'm only imagining them. Aren't I?

Too many coincidences replay in my head, and I rush to my room. My mind goes crazy, thinking over everything. Sometime during my deep thinking, Angel disappears for the day. Standing, I grab my purse and phone, slip on my shoes, then make my way down the stairs again.

With the door cracked, I listen and hear no voices or movement. I slip from the staircase and cautiously make my way to the front door. It must be some kind of miracle, but I manage to exit the house and gate without Gertrude becoming aware.

The air is damp with early morning perspiration as the sun slowly illuminates the receding fog. As I walk the streets, a few people wave, curiosity showing plainly on their faces. Once I reach the edge of town, I keep walking. The fog welcomes me with an embrace as I leave the mostly sleeping town behind. Too much has happened. What I just heard is the last straw. Nothing can hold me here anymore.

CHAPTER TWENTY

Betrayals

The pebbles in the rough street made of dirt dig into my butt and thighs through my jeans as I collapse in frustration. The tiny little town is fully alive now, as alive as the town can be. Three times I've entered the fog to leave. Each time it throws me right back here, later in the day than it should be. As of now, it looks like I've wasted half of the day in that fog with nothing to show for it. Why can't I leave?

The fog is thick, but I followed the edge of the road the whole time. I know I didn't get turned around. Maybe I'm not going crazy. Maybe I have never gotten well to begin with. Could this all be a terrible dream? Am I lying in some hospital bed, pumped full of drugs, and dreaming of a life going forward? Have I never left the nightmare?

That thought makes me sob, and I bury my face in my knees to cry. My entire body convulses with my intense sobs, and I hug my knees tighter. It's hopeless. Ava is right. I eventually lost myself.

"Emma?"

I tense at the familiar voice with the unfamiliar tone. As I lift my face from my knees, I curse my tear-stained cheeks and red eyes. Golden-brown eyes meet mine, but they are devoid of the warmth that normally radiates from them. I fight the urge to flinch away from that cold stare. Now the unknown connection between him and my employer is even more apparent in those deep pools.

"Why can't I leave?" I whisper.

His eyes harden further. "Why do you want to?"

I blink away welling tears. Edgar only stares at me, waiting for an answer. "Because this place scares me, and I am afraid I'm going crazy."

There. I said it. I will no longer hide who I am from him because I can no longer hide it from myself. I'm an insane woman with nothing to offer anyone, not even the golden boy of a town trapped in time. Everyone is better off with me gone.

"No," I whisper. "I'm not going crazy. I've been crazy for a long time."

His eyes change. Anger and hurt mold into confusion. "What do you mean? You seem perfectly normal to me."

I laugh. Not a soft chuckle or giggle but a hysterical cackle that I am unable to contain. Different tears trickle down my face as I laugh and cry at the same time. Finally, it ends, and I spend a little time trying to catch my breath. If he didn't believe I'm crazy before, he has to now.

Looking up at Edgar, I see those entrancing depths stuck on me. He seems uncertain. At the same time, he looks understanding. I cock my head to the side. "If you think I'm normal, you must be crazier than I am. I have never been normal."

"What do you mean?"

I sigh and look away, unable to meet those eyes I used to long to see. Telling him I'm crazy is one thing. Edgar should know of my insanity since he seems to be invested in charming me. He needs to know I'm broken, but I'm not sure I want him to know the specifics. That all seems too personal.

Instead, I try to change the subject. "I want the truth. Is that place haunted? Don't give me the runaround with cryptic answers! I've seen too much; I've heard too much."

Those beautiful eyes are cold again, but it is Edgar who looks away this time, refusing to answer my question. I purse my lips. "That is answer enough. Why did you lie to me?!"

Now he turns back, and I want to recoil from the anger I see on his face. He growls. "I never lie, and I didn't lie to you. I told you it's no more haunted than the rest of the town. I never told you it wasn't haunted!"

My eyes widen. So, it's not just the mansion. "Why didn't you tell me? On second thought, why do you constantly hedge my questions? It may not be lying, but it isn't much better."

His hands clench at his sides. "I have never been dishonest with you."

"No, but you have hidden things from me with vagueness."

"What do you want to know?"

I blink at his sudden change in tone. He almost sounds defeated, but not entirely. There is a stubbornness in Edgar, one I would love to get to know in another setting if we can ever forgive each other. "Why are you always so busy? Where do you go all day?"

"I help those around town as much as possible. I'm not so well-liked just because I'm a pretty face and come from money. I care about the town and its people. I do what I can to lessen their burden."

I'm taken aback. "Why didn't you tell me that?"

Edgar stares at me for a few moments. "I never omitted anything about what I do. If you would have asked outright again, your desire for knowledge would have been clearer. I would have told you of my less than glorious 'occupation' as the town favorite. Instead, you had to jump to conclusions, paint me as some evil liar."

My mouth falls open. Is that what I did? I think back. I remember him not answering my question clearly, but did I ever push the issue? I didn't, afraid to alienate the man I was developing feelings for. Instead of asking again, I accused him of hiding and lying just now. I am an idiot.

This time, I am the one defeated. "I'm sorry. I'm a broken person who shouldn't interact with others."

"Broken how?"

I break down in tears. In normal circumstances, I feel like Edgar would be on the ground comforting me, but I think I may have wounded him too much. Between sobs, I tell him of the nightmare and my sleepless nights. "Dying every single night has driven me over the edge. I'm not fit to be around others."

Silence meets my long confession. Looking up, I see his golden-brown eyes wide. That's it. I've done it now. My one ally in this place is now freaked out by me. So be it. I will do it alone. Do what alone?

"If this entire place is haunted, is it them that won't let me leave?"

No longer in shock, his eyes narrow again. "No, it isn't them."

He turns his back to me and takes a few steps. "You better get back to the mansion. Your employer knows you ran off and is none too happy."

"Who are you to him?"

Edgar freezes midstep. "Family."

"What happened to you?"

He begins walking again. "That isn't something I share with people who don't trust me."

I stand as he walks back toward town. Turning, I contemplate trying the fog one more time, but I know it's hopeless. There's not much more I can do. I'm trapped. Fighting tears, I walk back in the direction of the mansion.

Earlier, I had seen the town bustling. Now, as I pass through on my way back to my prison, everything is closed up and silent. Closed signs hang on shop doors. Not a soul is in sight. As if that isn't creepy enough, a feeling of terror hangs heavy in the air. I've never felt an emotion in the air before, but I can now. This is not a peaceful silence I am encountering. Fear radiates from the very essence of this little town.

The dark mansion looms ahead of me, and my feet feel heavier with each step. I've been missing most of the day. Edgar said that Master Radcliffe is upset with my disappearance. If he fires me, where can I go? I can't leave this town. I've alienated the only person I have befriended. What am I to do?

With a sigh, I approach the gate. It swings open as I draw near. Gertrude stands on the porch, hands firmly planted on her hips. My eyes widen at the sight of her. Apron hanging askew and her dark eyes glaring at me from beneath a bun that has lost control of strands of hair. Dark circles weigh down her eyes.

My perfectly made-up supervisor is in a very disheveled state. Movement catches my attention, and I turn in time to see a blond head retreat around the side of the house. Before he is gone, Isaac shoots me a pleased smirk.

My feet falter, wondering what in the world he is so pleased about. Was he expecting this? A rough clearing of Gertrude's throat snaps me back to the black-haired woman in front of me. She taps her foot and under normal circumstances, I'd probably laugh. Isaac is right. Gerty looks like a plump black chicken when she stands like that. I lick my lips and open my mouth.

Gertrude beats me to it. "Where have you been?!"

"I...uh...I just...um..."

"You left without a word, ignored your work, and left cheese and crumbs on the floor in the servants' kitchen. This is very unprofessional, and the master is very upset with you for running off!"

"I'm sorry, madame. I got a little weirded out, and I—"

"I don't want to hear your excuses! Get in there and clean. I don't care what, just as long as you do your job!"

Each word causes me to shrink within myself. "What about meals?"

"The master will not be eating today. He is too upset at his newest employee just up and running off."

"I'm not fired?" I venture.

I didn't think it would be possible, but her eyes harden further. "You should be, but no. He won't punish you."

I scurry past her, into the dark house. For some reason, her next whispered comment sends chills down my spine. "You won't pay for your actions, but others will."

CHAPTER TWENTY-ONE

Dead End Job

I stare up at the dark wood of the ceiling, ignoring the purring cat at my side. Another sleepless night behind me, I can't make myself move or care until absolutely necessary. Why should I even bother to care? I can no longer control what happens to me.

It's been three days since my unsuccessful attempts to flee. Master Radcliffe hasn't eaten in the dining room, and I haven't seen him around the gigantic house. Whenever I ask about him, Gertrude tells me he's not in a good mood and is out looking for ways to improve it; whatever that means. The snobbiness in her voice has only gotten worse when she speaks to me, as if she blames me for his foul mood. Why does what I do matter so much?

Edgar said that my employer knows I tried to run off, but how is that even possible? Maybe I just went into town. Even if it is possible, why does he care enough to rage and tantrum over it? I am only a house servant, completely replaceable.

Gertrude has made my life a living hell since my return. One would think the constant work would make it easier to sleep at night, but that one would be wrong. I've barely slept in days. My hopelessness does not induce sleep, and my dreams have only become more vivid. A notification chimes on my phone, and I reach over to see a text message from Ava.

Ava: Why haven't you called? I told you to call me! If you don't, I'm coming over there.

I sit straight up, dislodging the black ball of fur that is enjoying my warmth. After sending me a golden glare, Angel hops off the bed and stretches before slipping out the door I didn't even bother to latch. Why close the door? It's not like this place is safe at all. Ghosts don't care about doors.

My attention returns to my phone. As much as I would love to see my friend, I cannot stand the thought of her stuck in this old town as well, tortured by ghosts. Ghosts...

I have fully come to believe that is what I'm seeing. None of the other residents seem to be bothered by them, even though it is obvious they know, so I can't help but wonder why they're so attracted to me. Could this be the aura of fear I feel so heavily over this nervous little town? Edgar did say that the mansion is no more haunted than the rest of the town. Do they experience my torment as well?

I take a deep breath. These questions will get me nowhere, and I've alienated the one person who might have given me answers. No, Ava cannot come here. She must not. My best friend doesn't deserve to be stuck in this hell; I've caused her enough pain.

Me: I'm sorry. They've been keeping me busy, and I haven't had a free day in a while. Don't come here, please. I want to see you, but not here. I swear I will call as soon as I get the free time.

I'm relieved to see I have enough of a signal that the message goes through. Her little bubbles pop up, but then they disappear. I wait for them to show again. When they don't, I notice my signal is gone again and let out a frustrated groan.

I hope she listens. I will definitely call once I get a

chance. If I ever get the chance. Somehow I don't think Gertrude will be understanding of a request for a free day right now. She probably won't even trust my motives.

With a sigh, I get up to shower and start my day. Gertrude meets me at the bottom of the servants' stairwell. After thrusting a cart at me, she says, "Billiard room this time. You know the drill. There are also glasses to wash in the kitchen."

I hold back another sigh. This happens each day and night since I tried to escape, but the first night was the worst. Master Radcliffe has a very nasty temper and is throwing multiple tantrums every single day. Property is always broken and carpets soiled. I'm to clean up the mess, I guess because I am accused of causing it, and then document any damages for replacements.

I back the cart in through the door to the billiard room, slipping on something round on the floor. Pinwheeling my arms, I knock cleaning solution bottles off the top and tumble with them onto the floor. A crack sounds as whatever was under my foot propels toward the wall, and I lay on the floor for a few minutes doing nothing but groaning in pain.

Something round and hard is under my hip. My hand locates and pulls it out, bringing the black eight ball into view. I must have slipped on one of its companions. It was pretty stupid to walk into a room full of pool balls without looking after one of my employer's tantrums, but live and learn.

With an impressive moan, I roll over and lift myself to my feet. The balls are scattered all over the room, and the dark red velvet on the table is scratched and scarred. A few pool sticks are broken into two, the rest scattered all over the place. Rips scar the couches along the wall and the dark carpet beneath my feet. Holes that look suspiciously the same size as the balls mar the surface of the dark walls. Whiskey smells heavy when I step onto a squishy part of the carpet and grimace at the thought of it soaking into my shoes.

Impressive, but I've seen worse in the course of the last couple of days. Maybe his temper is finally dying down. One can hope at least. I'm not sure what more can be destroyed that hasn't already, but I don't want to make that a challenge for him.

Starting with the balls, I collect them and put them in the pockets. The top is trashed, so there is no point in setting them up like they usually are. I think I'm one ball short. While checking under the table, I hear something rolling behind me. Looking up, I see the missing ball roll out from under the butchered couch.

My heart stops at first, but then I just sigh. I might as well get used to this. "At least one of you is helpful," I mutter.

After putting the ball with the others, I begin using a rag to pull as much of the spilled whiskey out of the rug as possible and spray some cleaner on it. It takes some time, but I get most of the mess cleaned up. As I walk by the couch, my foot crunches on something. After moving the dark couch with a rough grunt, I find a shattered glass underneath and clean that up. Once the carpet is vacuumed, I make a list of damages and leave the billiard room.

Stacks of glasses, sticky with alcohol, fill the counter in the kitchen. My mouth drops, wondering why there are this many glasses in the mansion occupied by one person and why he is using so many. After squeezing some dish soap into the sink, I watch the water form bubbles and rise to the top, wishing I could use them to cleanse my dark thoughts.

Everything just feels hopeless, and I still question what is real.

The sound of a footstep slapping on tile makes me freeze. Slowly turning, I see the woman from my time hiding under the table behind me, halfway across the kitchen. A scream echoes from me, disgusted as her loose eye sways across her cheekbone. One bloody hand points at me and blood drips from the stumps of her fingers.

I back into the counter. Anger and frustration rise within me, and I decide I have had enough. "Why won't you leave me alone?"

She cocks her head to the side, her red hair sticking to her head with crimson stickiness. She opens her mouth, but only blood comes out. Why me? Why are they torturing me? I can't take this anymore. I can't run or fight, stuck in this town for who knows how long. Enough!

"Leave me alone!" I scream. My hand circles around one of the whiskey glasses. "I told you to go away!"

With all the power I possess, I yell and throw the glass at the bloody woman in front of me, squeezing my eyes shut so tight it hurts. The glass shatters, and I open my eyes. The woman is gone. The glass is broken all over the floor.

That was a smart move. Now, I have more shattered glass to clean up thanks to my volatile temper. As I dump the dustpan full of glass into the garbage, the sound of water hitting the floor grabs my attention. I turn, seeing the water overflowing from the sink and quickly forming an impressive puddle on the floor. I cry out in frustration, rushing over to turn the water off and unplug the drain. My feet slide across the floor as I carelessly walk to the closet to grab a mop.

Once I clean up my ever-growing messes, I bury my arms up to the elbows to wash the sticky glasses. After everything is clean and dry, I turn off the light and exit the kitchen. A strange sound reaches my ears, the sound of breathing. What now?

I turn in the direction of the sound. At the end of the dark hall, I see Master Radcliffe standing in the center and watching me. His raspy breathing echoes in the still air. The darkness down the hallway hides most of him, making him look even creepier than before. All I can see is his cane in front of him, both hands clutching the top of it, as well as his face. Everything else is in shadow.

Something about the way he watches me makes me shudder. "Master Radcliffe?"

Those golden-brown eyes stare at me intently, and he bangs his cane off the floor a few times, reminding me of the time I thought I saw him in my room. This time, there is no satisfied smile, only indifference and coldness. I swallow the lump in my throat.

"Sir," I try, "I'm sorry for the other day. I just got—"

My employer's back retreats down the hall, cane clicking with each step. He doesn't wait to hear my excuses, only continues into the darkness. This doesn't seem like a good sign.

CHAPTER TWENTY-TWO

Stolen Lists

I rub lotion over my wrinkled hands. It isn't until now that I realize how long my hands were in that sudsy water, washing glasses smelling of alcohol. No matter how hard I try, I cannot get the look on Master Radcliffe's face out of my mind. He looked very disappointed and unhappy. What have I done?

I can't afford to be fired. What would I do in this town without the job? Maybe they will let me leave then. Something deep within me says I am being stupid. I'm stuck here. There has to be some way out of this place.

I spend the night cuddling Angel, who seems to be the only one not mad at me for my attempted escape, and reading my latest book. When my alarm goes off, I get up, eat tasteless food, and get ready for another day of labor. I wonder which room is trashed today?

Angel meets me at the bottom of the stairs, raising my curiosity. The cat has never stuck around after I leave my room, but she's sitting in the hall watching me. I pause and watch as she cocks her head to the side before rolling on the carpet and meowing.

"What is it, Angel? I'm sure I have a busy day ahead of me."

Great, now I'm talking to a cat in the middle of the hall where anyone can see. I shake my head and walk to the closet. A list of chores waits on top of a cart. Looking over the list, I sigh. It is going to be a long day, but at least no meals today. I really don't want to face the master again. Something in those hard eyes makes me nervous to be around him, scared of what may happen.

As I turn to leave the cleaning closet, Angel jumps up and grabs the paper out of my hand. There was no reason to memorize any of it, so I need that list. I chase the black cat down the hall, shouting at her to give my itinerary back. Angel finally stops and drops my list of duties. Bending down, I pant for breath with my hands on my knees.

"Ever do that again, cat, and I'm going to turn into Gertrude on you."

I grab the piece of paper, and Angel rubs against my hand. When I stand, she stretches her front paws on the wall beside me. That's when I realize the cat led me down the forbidden hallway. I need to get out of here before anyone sees, or the thin ice I'm on is going to give way. Why didn't I pay attention to where I was going? It's not like losing the list is going to lower Gertrude's opinion of me any further.

Turning, I freeze, staring at the portrait over where Angel is scratching. My eyes widen at the woman in the picture. Her long red hair flows in thick curls over her shoulders, the same shade as mine. A black cat lays curled at her feet. Her eyes...

"Perfect shade of blue. Beautiful eyes. Look familiar?"

I cry out, covering my heart as I spin. Isaac stands there, his hands clasped behind his back. I have been caught. What more can go wrong today? "I didn't mean to come down this hall, I swear. Angel grabbed my list of duties, and I chased her. I didn't realize where I was heading until it was too late."

He chuckles. "Relax. I'm not Gerty."

The groundskeeper grabs my shoulders and turns me back to the picture on the wall. "Tell me what you see."

"A woman," I answer. "A black cat. Who is she?"

The strong grip releases my shoulders, and I turn back to ensure I hear the answer. Isaac takes a deep breath. "This is Amelia."

My eyes widen. This is the woman who keeps the town locked in grief. I turn back to Amelia's portrait. "I have heard that name many times. Who is she?"

He clears his throat. "She would have been the lady of the house eventually."

"What happened to her?"

I almost don't want to know, but if my coworker senses my hesitance, he ignores it. "It is a sad tale."

"What is going on here?!"

My eyes widen even further at the sound of that stuck-up voice. "Madame," I say, turning toward her voice. "I'm so sorry. I was chasing Angel and didn't know where I was."

Her eyes widen as she looks between me and the picture in shock that disappears quickly. An angry glare replaces all other emotion, and Isaac steps between us. "Relax, Gerty. It was a harmless mistake. It's not like she came here on purpose."

Gertrude huffs. "Don't call me that! It is Gertrude. How can you believe her after all the trouble she's caused? She's probably lying."

"I am not lying," I say in my defense. "What trouble have I caused?"

Gertrude's face turns red. "It's because of you that—"

Isaac clears his throat to stop her words. I am starting to get really tired of their many secrets. If I'm going to be stuck in this place, the least they can do is be honest with me. I deserve that much, no matter what Gertrude thinks. Before I can confront them, she turns on me.

"If you cannot follow simple orders, what use are you?! You were specifically told to never come down this hall. This will go on your record, and Master Radcliffe will be informed. I'm tempted to have the fleabag thrown in the nearest river! Since you cannot follow the simplest of orders, you are not needed today. You have the day off. Get out of my sight!"

I want to argue further, but Isaac shakes his head in warning. I run back to my room, fighting tears the whole way. I've done it now. Soon, I'll be wandering around this town with nothing left. My job will not survive all my screw-ups, but I can't leave. If they fire me, I'll try to navigate the fog again, but it might just be an endless and hopeless cycle. What am I to do?

The picture on my dresser pulls my eyes. Talking may help my anxiety. I change out of my work dress and release my pinned-up hair before heading out of my extravagant prison.

As I traverse the streets, those around me avert their eyes. Some show fear, but others wear a look that reminds me of disappointment. Why are they scared of me? What have I done to make them disappointed in me? I barely know these people.

My mind takes me back to my initial walk through this tiny village nestled between the hills. I felt less than welcome back then, but it now feels worse than when I first arrived. What have I done to earn this treatment?

As I get closer to the phone booth, I look through my bag. I don't have much change. The looks I am receiving make me feel like I won't be accepted in many places. Looking around, I see the seamstress shop ahead. With a resigned huff, I figure this will be my best bet and walk through the door, flinching at the chime of the bell overhead.

The owner looks over at me, her smile falling when she sees who has entered her small shop. She flattens her lips before giving me an unconvincing smile. Maybe I misjudged. Even she is upset with me for whatever I did wrong.

"I'm sorry to bother you," I say. "Can you please give me some change for a few dollars?"

I dig a few dollar bills out of my bag and hold them out. She looks at me, debating whether to fulfill my request. My nerves begin to act up, wondering what in the world is going on. Why am I being treated like this? Our previous encounters have been strained, but I knew it wasn't me. This time, it's definitely me.

Without a word, she grabs the dollars out of my waiting hands and slides the appropriate change across the counter. I thank her but only receive a muttered reply as I leave. I sigh, walk out the door, then make my way to the phone booth.

The door clangs as I confine myself into the tiny space, locking myself away from the stares of the townspeople. After three rings, I hear my best friend's voice on the other end. "Emma?"

"Yeah, it's me."

"Emma! I've been worried sick. You can't just send me a message like that and not respond!"

I sigh, twirling the coiled metal that connects the

receiver to the old phone. "It's not like I can respond with any kind of reliability, Ava."

"I don't care," she says. "If you need to send smoke signals, then do it! I've been so worried about you."

"I swear I'm fine. I was just having a bad day."

Silence meets me from the other end. "Okay," I admit, "my bad days may be scary. This isn't like that."

Ava hesitates but asks, "Then why does your voice sound so lost?"

I groan and lean my head against the side of the booth. Having a friend this great is something I cherish and would never trade for anything, but having someone know you well enough to tell everything you are trying to hide just by your tone can be rough.

"I'm just tired," I say, then realize how that's going to sound.

Ava proves me right. "Are you not sleeping again? You told me you would get medicine and see someone if needed."

Tears threaten. What can anyone do for me right now? I lie. "I swear I'm looking for one. Please don't worry. I'll see if I can get a few days off, and maybe we can meet halfway or something for a weekend sometime."

If the town will ever let me.

I can't voice that without risking my best friend. How can I keep stalling her? She needs to stay away from this place. It's Ava's turn to sigh. "Fine. Call me when you get another day off though. I don't want to go so long without hearing from you."

"I promise," I say, wondering if I'll even have a job soon. I wonder if I can fake it to keep her away. The phone gives me the low-time warning. "Love ya, Ava. I have to go. I'm out of change."

"Alright. Love you too, Emma. Please take care."

The phone cuts us off. I slide a couple of quarters around in my fingers, feeling a little guilty for the lie. Ava can be pushy, and I don't blame her at all. I just don't like being a burden and don't feel I could have hidden it much longer.

A squeak echoes in my tiny phone box. Turning, I jump and look around. The glass of the booth is fogged, the name "Amelia" written within the cloud. I run my hand over the name, wiping it from the glass.

This was done from inside the booth.

CHAPTER TWENTY-THREE

One-sided Conversation

The waitress drops my turkey club on the table in front of me, throwing me an icy stare before walking away. I hope she didn't spit in my sandwich. Peter would be furious; I'm sure of it. Edgar sits across from me, his eyes glued onto his cheeseburger. I met him outside the phone booth. He asked to talk to me, but so far, he hasn't been very chatty.

After our talk on the road out of town, it feels like a brick wall has been built between us. Awkwardness is an uninvited companion to this lunch. I feel bad for the way our last conversation went, but could it really have gone any other way? I'm a neurotic mess, and he isn't incredibly truthful with me.

I take a bite of my hopefully spit-free sandwich, mayonnaise smearing over my lips. Embarrassed, I grab my napkin and wipe it off. The man across from me nibbles on a fry and remains silent. The silence is killing me, and I decide I've had enough. "You ask me to talk and then say nothing. By the way, I plan on paying for my own lunch this time."

His golden-brown eyes finally fly up. "That wouldn't be proper."

"I don't care what is proper," I counter. "I'm a grown woman and can pay for my own lunch. It's not like we are on a date. This is a talk that has so far been silent."

He goes back to his food and takes an angry bite of his

burger as if chewing is a release of pent-up frustration. I try not to smile. He's cute when he's sulking. Shaking my head, I ask myself what I'm thinking. It isn't like our relationship is in a good place right now. I accused him of lying to me, and he admitted to not being completely open with me.

I'm sure with time, I could get him to open up, but I am pretty sure I ruined that chance by calling him a liar. Edgar was my only true ally, and I managed to screw that up. Looking back up at the man across the table, I find his entrancing eyes examining me.

With a sigh, Edgar swallows his bite and sits back. "Our last encounter did not go well. I apologize for being cold. I thought you were running out on me."

I put my sandwich down and wipe my fingers on my napkin. "To be truthful, I was."

His eyes drop, and I can tell he's contemplating how to get away right now. I hurry on. "I wasn't running from you. Strange things happened in the house that freaked me out pretty badly, so I was frightened and tried to run away from the situation. It isn't you."

Edgar meets my gaze again. "Ghosts? Is that why you asked me?"

I sigh, deciding to just let it all out. "Yes. I've been seeing some really frightening things lately. At first, I thought it was because I wasn't sleeping, but too much happened for me to believe that anymore. That's why I was so adamant on getting the truth."

I pause and take a deep breath. "I'm sorry. I didn't mean to call you a liar. It's just... Well, I never really pushed you for an answer because I was afraid to push you away. My life has been full of pushing people I care about away. You are the only friendly person in this town, besides Peter, who I only ever get to see when Master Radcliffe is in the mood to eat."

He purses his lips. "That's only because you won't let others in. I know these people are a bit reclusive. They have their reasons. If you would try to be a little friendlier, you may be surprised at how joyful these people can be."

Edgar is right. I have never truly given this town a chance. From the beginning, all I have done is judged how out of touch and quiet the people are. I look up to see Edgar watching me in thought. "What?"

Golden-brown eyes stare at me for a little while longer, then apprehension takes over his gaze. "I'm sorry. I have to go."

"What? We aren't done talking."

"I'm sorry, Emma. There's just something I need to do."

Throwing a mass of money onto the table, he gets up and practically runs out of the diner, leaving his meal only half-eaten. When I see that he has thrown down enough for both sandwiches, I growl. My lunch no longer looks appetizing, but I won't waste his money.

THE WALK out of the town is no better than the walk in was, but I still try to smile at those I pass. If I am going to be stuck here, these people will be all I know. Edgar was right when he said I have never tried to get to know them.

Exhausted by trying to be friendly and being rejected, I walk up the road to the mansion, wondering what my reception will be. It is still early afternoon, but I can't take the stares any longer. My mind has continually returned to what happened earlier.

I've heard so much about Amelia and have gathered that she was beloved by the town. Nothing else is really apparent. Edgar seems to know a lot, but our conversation was cut short by his random and weird reaction before he made a run for it.

We may not be on the best of terms right now, but I thought the whole point of the lunch was to maybe clear the air a little. His abrupt departure is both confusing and infuriating. I need answers.

The squealing of the gate pulls me from my thoughts, and I look up at the dark mansion before me. Isaac seems to be willing to say more than anyone else. Maybe that's a good place to start.

Circling the house, I search for the lone groundskeeper. I find him in the back, within a grove of dead trees that can be seen from the gate. Isaac sprinkles something over the dirt around the trees.

He sees me and stops. "You have a habit of ending up in places you shouldn't be."

I sigh, looking down at my feet. "I'm sorry if I got you in trouble. I don't think it matters really. Gertrude will tell Master Radcliffe what I did, and I'll be jobless."

The breeze lifts his blond hair as he cocks his head. "I highly doubt that," he mumbles.

"What do you mean?"

Isaac clears his throat and tosses more from the bag onto the dry-looking soil around the dead trees. "No reason. Don't worry, I won't tell anyone you're back here. Ole Gerty doesn't bother me."

"Isn't she in charge around here?"

The groundskeeper chuckles so loud I jump back, startled at the sound. He looks back up at me. "That old hen?

She couldn't do anything to me. No one else is able to keep the grounds and house as I can."

After sprinkling the ground of the tree in front of me, he puts the bag down. "Is there a reason you came back here?"

I look at the unmarked sack. "Is that fertilizer?"

"Of a sort."

This makes no sense. "What good is fertilizing dead trees?"

Isaac runs a hand over rough bark. "These trees are special. They are here to honor those that came before. I'm glad I won't have to plant one for you."

My eyes narrow. "The ones who came before? The women hired before me?"

He nods. "Each one has a special soul."

This conversation is getting a little creepy. "Weren't they fired and just left?"

"They weren't to the master's liking and were let go. I feel bad for those girls. Something of them will always remain."

I'm really not liking how this conversation is going. Were they trapped here too? Why haven't I seen one of them? I decide to change the subject. "The woman in the portrait..."

"Amelia."

"Yes, Amelia. Who exactly was she? I'm assuming she has great importance to be hanging in the forbidden hallway."

Isaac sighs. "Love does strange things to a man. Doesn't it?"

Now I'm really confused. Only one thing makes sense here. "Master Radcliffe loved her?"

He sidesteps my question once again. "We get one true love in life, I believe."

I try something else. "What happened to her?"

"She died."

Well, that was a bit blunt. "I figured that, but how did she die?"

Isaac is silent for a while, often fidgeting. He looks nervous. "She was the light of this place. The townspeople loved her so dearly; they still do. Even her laughter was enough to lighten the mood. Everything fell apart after the town lost her."

"What happened to her?"

Blue eyes meet mine. "I need to get back to work. Enjoy the rest of your day off. I bet Gerty will be annoying tomorrow after what happened today. You should get back before she notices you are where you shouldn't be again."

"But—"

He walks away without another glance. That man is so strange.

There is no sign of Gertrude when I enter the house. As quiet as I can be, I climb the main staircase. At the top, I stare into the dark and forbidden hallway, curious to know more about the mysterious Amelia. With a sigh of resignation, I admit it will probably never happen and head upstairs.

I wish to avoid Gertrude and her tight black bun until I have no choice but to confront her. Angel is nowhere in sight when I enter my room, so I sit alone on my bed. My book is almost done, but I lean back and try to lose myself in the ending of the story.

While staring at the back cover, I reflect on my chances of getting back to the library without being seen. I am not confident in those chances. Instead, I pull out the romance novel I didn't think I'd like and start it again.

CHAPTER TWENTY-FOUR

Violent Reprimands

The ticking of the giant grandfather clock is the only other sound other than the scraping of silverware over fancy china. Pure agonizing silence is only accentuated by the cold glares Gertrude sends at me from her perch by the door to the hall. Master Radcliffe has not looked at me once, and I'm happy to keep it that way.

Breakfast this morning is the first time I've seen my employer since I tried to escape. Well, besides the strange encounter in the dark hall, but I'm not counting that one. I don't even want to remember it.

"Dessert!"

I nearly jump, my heart hammering in my panicked chest. Master Radcliffe gazes at me with those disturbing eyes. I grab the plate holding one of Amelia's Tears, trying not to shudder at the name that now makes me uncomfortable, and place the dessert plate on the serving one after removing his breakfast dish with my empty hand.

With steady hands that amaze me, I place the soiled plate and silverware on the serving tray and resume my position by the kitchen door. My employer finishes his delectable dessert and stands. Gertrude hurries over with his hat and cane.

Once they're out of sight, I begin to clear the table. "Master Radcliffe," I hear in a low mumble.

Glancing at the door, I notice it's not closed the whole way. I debate on whether I should go over and close it. If they are right on the other side, my intrusion would not be welcome. With a deep breath, I go back to my task but keep my ears open. Eavesdropping is becoming a dangerous habit of mine. How else am I to get answers?

"What is it, Gertrude?" As always, Master Radcliffe's raspy voice makes me shiver. Since he is no longer in sight, I allow the sensation to show.

"I don't understand why you have not punished Miss Blackwood for being where she was clearly forbidden to be. She broke a rule. Others have not been spared before." Gertrude rambles, trying to get all of this out as fast as possible. She is probably afraid to keep him waiting longer than necessary.

Listening is terribly rude, but I can't help myself. I have been wondering this exact same question. Although, I can't help but wonder about the "others have not been spared." That sounds pretty ominous.

The raspy voice makes my teeth clench. "You said she claims to have been led there by the cat."

"I don't know why it matters that the flea-ridden beast took her there, she—"

"Careful how you speak of the cat, Gertrude. You know she is dear to me." The warning is clear in that tone, and despite my dislike of the woman with the black bun, I hope she takes it.

The dishes very quietly make their way to the cart, and I walk to the kitchen door to open it. I stop there, unwilling to miss the conversation about my future.

"I'm s-sorry, sir. I just don't understand."

An annoyed, gruff sigh barely reaches my ears. "It is a sign. Enough of this."

"But, sir—"

"I said enough!" Master Radcliffe growls. "I am still your employer, and you will not argue further. Do not make me angry. Get back to work."

The clicking of his cane fades as he walks away. I slip into the kitchen as quietly as possible, careful to not alert the most likely angry woman right in the hall. The dishes clatter in the sink as I mix soap and water. I drag the heavy pans and pots over and set them to soak.

Startled by the sound of the kitchen door, I see Gertrude walking in, a tray of liquor glasses in her hands. Without looking at me, she places them on the counter next to the bubbly sink, followed by the tray.

"When you are finished here, Miss Blackwood, I expect you to vacuum all the carpets in the halls and rooms, except where you have been told to avoid. Do not let me find you where you do not belong again."

"Yes, madame," I mutter a hasty reply.

She tosses me a sneer, then leaves the kitchen. From the overheard conversation, I gather Master Radcliffe wants me to stay, but Gertrude doesn't want me here anymore. While happy to still have a place to live, I worry about the anger my direct supervisor has for me. Is there something I can do to make her more amiable toward me?

Putting the last plate to dry, I slip the glasses into the water full of bubbles, one by one. When I reach for the last one, my hand meets only air. The counter next to the sink is empty, and I search with my eyes, confused and sure there was another glass. I find it on the other end of the counter.

"If I stop being scared, will you get bored and go away because I'm tired of this?" Of course, there is no answer. "Can't you at least be as helpful as the one who found the billiard ball for me?"

My eyes widen as the glass slides over the counter, faster as it comes nearer. It flies into the sink with so much force that it shatters, making me cry out in surprise. Next, the pot of soapy water is knocked to the floor, then silence.

I've told myself not to be scared of the ghosts anymore, since I need to live with them, but that freaked me out a bit. Here I had been hoping they'd get bored and leave me alone. Instead, I'm met with anger. I should have considered that reaction.

With a sigh, I grab a few towels and dry up the greasy water covering the floor and place the pot back on the counter. I will need to mop, but I'll finish the dishes first. Turning back to the sink, I'm faced with a different dilemma. There's shattered glass in the murky water. I grab a serving spoon and scrape the sink until the drain plug lifts.

I remove the slick glasses, avoiding the broken shards buried in them. Once unharmed glasses are removed, I gingerly pick out the shards. My grip slips, getting cut by a particularly large sliver. Instinct causes my finger to go into my mouth, and I grimace at the soapy booze taste I now have on my tongue. After wrapping my bleeding digit in a towel, I clean the rest of the glass up and go in search of a mop.

I stop at one of the bathrooms to grab a first aid kit to bandage my finger before finding a mop and bucket. The floor is cleaned, then I finish washing the dishes, hissing whenever soapy water touches my cut finger.

VACUUMING IS hard with a slice in a finger, but I manage and am careful to avoid the forbidden hallway. It has taken me all day, so I'm glad I have no other meals to serve. Sore and tired, I climb the stairs to the servant's hallway.

My hair cascades down my back, and I moan in relief. I look around my room but see no sign of the black cat and find myself missing her. I am sure she will turn up. What did Master Radcliffe mean by being fond of her? I never took him for an animal lover. In the end, I file this knowledge away with everything else that makes no sense.

After changing into something more comfortable, I make my way to the kitchen for something to eat. Nothing in the fridge looks appealing, but I'm starving after working myself into a sweat all day, so I grab something at random. As I stand up and close the refrigerator door, I jump and drop the foiled packet of food. Gertrude stands in the doorway, eyeing me with what I can only describe as pure and unhidden hatred.

I gulp. "Can I help you, Madame? I finished my chores and am feeling a bit hungry. Is there something else?"

"I don't know who you think you are," she growls.

"Excuse me?" What is she talking about? I begin to feel extremely uncomfortable as her dark glare becomes even harsher.

"I have a nice setup here. You have to come along and ruin it. It is not right. I am the one who has been here for him all this time."

What is she going on about? Has Gerty finally lost it? If she has, I can't blame her at all after my short time here. This place can make anyone crazy, and she's been here much longer than I have.

Gertrude takes a step toward me. Her stance and posture make me take a step back. When she's by the knife block, she grabs a large blade, and my eyes widen. Nothing can take my eyes off the gleam of that sharp knife.

"Madame?" My voice shakes, but she only stares at me with frigid coldness.

With a speed I would've never thought she possesses, Gertrude lunges at me with the knife. I scream, jump back, trip over my own feet, then fall backward. I try to stand, but she is right on top of me. I fight off the knife, ending up with a cut in my left forearm.

Frantic, I struggle with all I have as the pointy end of the knife shines right in front of my face. Blood runs down my arm, but I dare not take my eyes off the crazed woman above me. Somehow, in this frantic moment, I notice wisps of hair have loosened from her black bun in our struggle.

The knife is so close that I have to cross my eyes to see the point; not that I want to. Pain radiates all through my arm as blood stains my shirt. When I feel I can't hold her back anymore, Gertrude cries out and pulls away from me, the knife clattering to the floor. I scramble backward, sliding in my own blood pooling all over the once-clean floor.

Managing to stand, I look back to see the crazy woman fighting to get a black cat that blends in with her black dress off her back. Feeling a little guilty, I let Angel fight this battle and flee. The stairwell door is locked, and sounds of anger and growling come from the kitchen behind me.

I run down the hall and into the bathroom, quick to lock the door behind me. I stare at the door for a while, startled when I hear banging on the other side. Gertrude curses me, then all is silent. It takes a while to remember the cut on my arm.

I wash the open wound in the sink, not caring enough to clean up the mess I make. Grabbing a towel, I sit with my back against the tub with the fluffy cloth wrapped around my forearm and apply pressure. I don't take my eyes from that door.

CHAPTER TWENTY-FIVE

Trust Issues

Sometime during the night, I fell asleep. A knock on the door jerks me from my dark dreams before the knife sinks into me. I breathe for a few seconds, feeling the cold bathroom tile pressing into my cheek. Disorientation makes my head swirl. The knock sounds again, louder this time.

My eyes widen as the events of last night come back to me. I look around for any kind of weapon but find none. I can't even blind her with cleaning spray or beat her with a plunger. Cleaning supplies have no place outside the cleaning closet unless in use. Maybe I could stab her with a toothbrush.

Breathing ragged, I wonder if I should hold the door. The knock sounds again. "Miss Emma?"

My mouth drops. "Isaac?" I croak.

I need to repeat myself a few times because my throat is dry and raw, but I eventually gain enough volume to pass through the closed door.

"Yes, it's me."

Do I dare trust him? Yeah, he has only been somewhat kind to me, if maybe a little creepy. Nothing I have seen would make me think he is out to hurt me. Then again, I didn't think Gertrude would ever come after me with a knife. "What do you want?"

"Your shift starts soon. Master Radcliffe sent me to check on you. I heard what happened. Let me help. Are you hurt?"

I chew on my lip. "How do I know I can trust you?"

"I guess you don't," he admits. "But you can't stay hidden in the bathroom until you die. I promise I won't hurt you. What do you need?"

I lift my arms to my face, then wince. "A first aid kit would be a step in the right direction. Maybe some water."

Footsteps recede as I contemplate my next move. He's right. I can't hide here forever. Escaping doesn't seem to be an option either. Where would I even go? It isn't like I have any friends that would hide me, and I can't leave the town.

Isaac knocks again. With reluctant resignation, I unlock the door and step back. Isaac walks in with a bottle of water and a first aid kit. I gulp the water down, my dry throat grateful.

Isaac looks me over. "Where are you hurt?"

I lift my arm and watch him flinch from the bloody towel wrapped around it. With a gentleness I would have never expected from the rough handyman, he starts to unwrap the towel, mumbling about how stupid Gerty is.

The towel is stuck to my wound, and I yelp in pain. Isaac sighs and steps back. "It might be a good idea to get in the shower and let the water soften the blood. I don't want to make it start bleeding again by yanking it off. I'll wait outside. Get in the shower, gently remove the towel, and clean up. I'll be in when you're done."

I stare at the door after he leaves. In complete disbelief, I look at the blood-soaked towel hanging from my arm, then follow his instructions. It takes a lot of water and some coaxing, but I manage to get the towel off without further damage and clean up. The water and soap sting, but Isaac is right that it needs to be cleaned.

Once out, I wrap another towel around me and tell him to come back in. The groundskeeper enters again with a blanket in his hands. He tells me to sit and lets me cover my lap with the rough fabric.

Isaac examines my wound. "It's not so deep that it needs stitches, but I'll clean it more and add some antiseptic."

He does as he says and wraps my arm in a tight bandage. I can't take it any longer. "How do you know what happened?"

"Master Radcliffe was searching for Gertrude and found her beating on the bathroom door with a bloody knife. She has been severely punished and is not allowed around you any longer. I am to deliver your duty lists to you."

My eyes narrow. "She tried to kill me. If it wasn't for Angel, I might be dead right now. Why should I stay?"

He shakes his head. "You know as well as I do that you cannot leave."

"Did you know I was listening that morning?"

Isaac pauses, but then tapes the bandage off and looks into my eyes. "You are safe, Miss Emma."

Realizing another question will remain unanswered, I ask, "Why did she try to kill me? Is Angel alright?"

"Gertrude is often frustrating, but I never thought of her as stupid," he says with a sigh. "As for her reasoning, only she could tell you, but I suggest avoiding her. She shouldn't be stupid enough to try something again. Then again, I didn't expect her to be this much of an idiot in the first place. The cat is fine, definitely won that fight."

"I don't feel comfortable working here anymore, Isaac."

His blue eyes meet mine. "I'm not sure you have much of a choice, but I *am* sure you already know that. Get dressed. The master wants you to serve breakfast, which is in fifteen minutes. I wouldn't make him angry; well, angrier. After that, he wants you to just rest in your room. He figures you need some time after last night."

Isaac doesn't give me time to argue before standing and walking out the door. How can one man be so creepy and caring at the same time?

PUTTING my stiff dress on is pretty painful, but I manage to by carefully watching my injured arm. Pulling my hair up in a tight bun is a bit difficult. I somehow manage. Flexing my arm, I sigh. This is going to be a long meal.

A black ball of fur startles me as Angel leaps onto my bed. Yellow eyes stare up at me. "Angel!"

Without reservation for my injured arm, I scoop the black cat up and hug her to my chest. To my surprise, she doesn't fight and simply purrs. A rough tongue caresses my chin, and I smile in happiness.

I place her back on my bed and look her over. "Did that evil woman hurt you?"

Angel gives me a reassuring meow, but I check her over thoroughly. "Thank you for saving me. I don't know what would have happened if you weren't there. I'm so glad you're okay."

She purrs and rubs against my hand. As much as I want to stay and snuggle with my savior, I have work I have to do.

Peter is already present in the kitchen when I enter. With a huge smile, he turns to me, but that smile disappears when he notices the bandages on my arm. He runs over. "Oh my! What happened?"

"It was only an accident," I lie.

The cook looks at me with skepticism but only sighs. "I hope it isn't too bad, my dear. Are you alright to work?"

I stare at the gentle man before me. All the coldness that I have received from the town lately has made me forget what a kind man Peter is. Even this tiny bit of sympathy means the world to me in this dark time. Trying to smile, I realize it isn't working very well and burst out into tears instead.

A startled cook looks on before patting my back awkwardly and trying to murmur words of comfort that aren't that comforting. We are interrupted by the clock chiming the breakfast hour in the other room. Peter jumps up and runs for the door. "I'm sorry to have to run, my dear. You know the drill."

I sigh and wish him a good day, frustrated and angry that this place forces me to live in such isolation in my times of need. With a deep breath, I place the fancy dish of food on the tray and walk through the door. To my relief, Gertrude is nowhere in sight, and I breathe out a deep breath I didn't realize I was holding. I don't know how I'd react to seeing her right now.

After setting the plate of breakfast goodies on the serving dish, I move to walk back to my place. A cool, wrinkled hand circles my wrist with a strength I would never expect from an old man with a cane. I meet my employer's eyes.

Master Radcliffe observes me for a while without moving his hand away, and I quickly look down. His raspy voice says, "Why are your eyes red?"

I press my lips together before replying, "Must be allergies, sir."

Master Radcliffe's hand tightens, and I try not to wince when I feel the bones in my wrist shift. How is he this strong? "Do not lie to me, Miss Blackwood."

I clear my throat. "I'm just not entirely comfortable working a normal day like nothing happened after the woman overseeing my work tried to kill me."

Hearing how angry my voice sounds, I brace for an outburst of a man who doesn't like to be questioned. "Ah," he says, turning cheerful. "You do not need to worry. She has learned her lesson well. Besides, it is not a normal workday. I have given you the rest of the day to recover in your room. You may take multiple books from the library if you would like."

How kind of him. Assuming it would not go over well, I try not to roll my eyes. Instead, I thank him and turn to take up my position.

"You don't believe me?"

I freeze at his words. Angering the only person keeping Gertrude from my throat wouldn't be smart. "It's not that, sir. I'm just pretty shaken up."

"Look here."

I turn but avoid those disturbingly cold eyes. He slides a key across the table. "Lock the stairwell door if you would like. Gertrude no longer has access."

"Thank you, sir," I mutter, taking the key with a shaking hand.

We spend the rest of the meal in silence. Once his plate is empty, he sits in his chair, making no move to leave. Master Radcliffe uses a throat clear to grab my attention, then nods in the direction of the doorway. It takes a second to realize what he wants, and I hurry over to grab his hat and cane.

As he adjusts his hat, I hold the smooth cane top in my palms, feeling the coolness of the worn wood in my hands. He takes the old walking stick from me, then leaves, his cane clicking down the hall. I close the door before starting my task of cleaning up.

CHAPTER TWENTY-SIX

Not in the Job Description

I spend my day and night reading a number of books that I picked up on the way back to my room. The key shines in the low light next to my phone. After making sure the door was shut and locked tight, I had come in here and not moved from my bed except to eat and use the bathroom.

Heat radiates from the black ball of fur laying against my leg. One hand absently strokes her softness, and she has no intention of moving any more than she needs to when she shifts position. Purrs are music to my ears and offer ample reward for my continued attention. From time to time, Angel opens her eyes long enough to give me a head-butt and a small lick on my fingers. Ignoring the near-death experience and being trapped here, this is a great way to spend a day.

Suppertime draws near, and my stomach gives a low rumble. As much as I don't want to end this cuddle session, I need to get some food in me. Angel doesn't move as I slide from bed, only stretches with a big yawn and lays her head back down. I believe she trusts me to return.

I find a marinated chicken breast in the refrigerator from Peter. I warm it, filling the kitchen with the smell of garlic and other spices, then place it between two slices of fresh-baked bread. After grabbing a bag of chips, I walk back to my room. The smell of chicken perks up the cat on my bed. With a small meow, she sits up and eyes me with such extreme interest that I can't hold back a laugh.

I share my sandwich and go back to reading. At some point, Angel leaves. She isn't gone long and returns to my side. We pass the entire night away together.

Morning comes too fast, and my burning eyes cry for a rest. I still dare not sleep. After a quick shower, I wrap fresh bandages around my sore arm and get dressed. When I approach the stairs, I notice a slip of paper on the floor. Opening it, I see a list of duties in a different hand than I'm used to.

Isaac must have written this list, then slid it under the door when he found it locked. Looks like I'm doing windows today. Once I have a cart and a stepladder, I begin to go from room to room and throw back all the heavy, dark drapes.

Beautiful outside light streams through the dense clouds and illuminates each area until I finish. It's amazing how much different this place looks with just a tiny bit of light. Even the cloudy sky manages to light up the room much more than it was. My rag squeaks over each pane as I slowly wipe it over the glass after a good spray of cleaner.

I'm careful to only use my uninjured arm as I clean the window to leave as little streaking as possible with minimal pain. While I've been told that Gertrude is no longer a danger, I know that Master Radcliffe would be upset if I failed to do my job properly. He isn't a man I want to anger any further.

Moving from room to room, I make the windows sparkle, then cover them with heavy drapes. This all seems pointless to me. What is the point of clean windows that are never allowed to let the light in? As I clean the library windows, I notice the sky is getting darker. Looks like some wicked rain is moving in, making me grateful for the roof over my head, even if it's full of ghosts and murderous women with tight buns.

I move my step ladder to the next window in the library. As soon as I go to climb on it, it's shoved out from under my feet and thrown across the room. With a loud thud, I land on my stomach and glare at the offending piece of furniture while hissing at the pain in my arm. "Would you guys just leave me alone? Haven't I been through enough?"

Silence answers me, and I sigh. This time, I'm able to climb up and start cleaning the window from the top down. When I get to the bottom, I look up to see fingerprints spontaneously show up all over the top panes.

"Really? You should have something better to do than torture a helpless woman who is already injured and doesn't want to be here."

I climb back up and clean the smudges again. As I replace the drapes, I see them reappear. "Fine. Leave it like that. If asked, I know who to blame."

With a huff, I stomp out of the library and move to the entryway. The windows along the door are much easier to wipe down, no climbing necessary. For good measure, I walk outside and clean there. I may not be able to do the outside of the other windows, but I can get these ones.

"Emma?" Turning, I see Isaac halfway between the porch and the gate. "I can get the outside."

"I know," I reply, finishing up the last one. "I just thought it would be nice to step out for a quick minute and be able to get both sides clean on at least one set of windows. Is that going to get me in trouble?"

He laughs. "Not at all. Come here. Let me check your bandages."

"I cleaned the wound thoroughly this morning and put fresh bandages on it."

"I figured you would," he admits, "but I want to make sure it's healing well."

With a nod, I agree to give him peace of mind. He slides a screwdriver into his belt, wipes his hands clean, then unwraps my arm. "Looks good."

"I told you," I mutter, but he only chuckles.

"What is going on out here?" Hearing that voice sends fear coursing through me. Turning, I see Gertrude glaring hatred at me. I gulp and back up right into Isaac.

He growls behind me. "I am checking on the damage your stupidity caused."

"My stupidity? The only stupid thing going on is still welcoming this troublemaker." Her eyes never leave me, and I begin to tremble.

"Gerty, move away. Haven't you caused enough trouble? Do you want to be punished again?"

Fear flashes in her dark eyes, and I wonder what was done to her to earn that reaction. Thunder echoes in the sky above, still distant but not too far. The hatred returns to Gertrude's eyes tenfold, replacing the fear I saw for a moment.

"Leave it be," Isaac warns. "Step away and go back to your duties."

"Do you really want things to go this way, Isaac? It has been only us for so long. You want to give that up?"

He sighs. "If it brings the town peace, I would be happy. What about you? Where is your selfish head going, trying to push the people into further torment?"

What is he talking about? Peace? What kind of peace could even be possible in this miserable town? Everyone seems to be full of fear and anxiety. Thunder makes me jump, closer now. The angry sky gets darker, and I see a bright flash of lightning light up the grayness. This is not the place for this argument, but there is no way I'm going to try to get around Gertrude. I won't give her another shot at me.

"Selfish, am I?" Gertrude speaks to Isaac without taking her eyes off me. "Do you really think it will change anything? I, for one, highly doubt it, and you should too. It will never change, even with her here. Enough of this!"

She lunges at me, and I reach for Isaac behind me. As I'm knocked to the ground, Gertrude's weight on top of me, I feel something dislodge from his belt. He yells for her to stop, and I fight to keep her from my throat. My hands grasp the screwdriver that I removed from Isaac's belt as I fell. With all the strength I possess, I thrust it into Gertrude's side.

She stands quickly, using words I never expected a proper woman like her to utter. Despite the screwdriver sticking out of her side, she doesn't flinch or cry out. I scramble to my feet as she pulls it out and glares at me.

Isaac steps between us. "That may not have been the smartest move, Emma. I would have gotten her off you."

I stare at the woman throwing the screwdriver to the side and muttering about the hole in her dress. "I stabbed her. She should be hurting or dead."

The darkness in Isaac's chuckle makes me take a step back, no longer feeling safe in his presence. Gertrude lunges at me again, but he holds her back. "Dead? You can't kill something that is already dead."

My eyes widen as his words sink in. He can't mean...

"This is not in the job description," I whisper.

Without another thought, I turn and run, listening to Gertrude cackling behind me and Isaac cursing at her.

Nothing stops my feet, not even when the sky opens up and soaks me within seconds. I can't stop.

None of this can be real. I have to be dreaming. Right now, the thought of being raving mad in some hospital bed while hallucinating everything going on is preferable to believing any of this is true. She can't already be dead. That makes no sense, but my mind keeps replaying the screwdriver incident over and over.

Tears stream down my face, hidden by the rain coming from above. I scream; the thunder drowns out all sound. My feet continue to run, splashing in the mud of the unpaved road. I look back and am stop when I hit something solid.

Strong arms grab me as I stumble, and I scream and fight. None of this is real This can't be happening. "Emma! It's me!"

The only voice that could stop my headlong rush into and away from the unknown reaches me through the storm. Edgar stands in front of me, his golden-brown eyes pleading for me to listen. His rich clothes cling to him in the rain, and his hands keep my shoulders trapped.

"Edgar? What is going on?! You said you won't lie to me, but there is no way you didn't know!!!"

I feel like a madwoman, screaming at the one man that can make me understand, but I need answers. Only he can give me the answers I seek. He flinches. "This town is not as it seems."

"No shit!" I scream, startling the sophisticated man before me. "Tell me what is going on. Is she really dead?!"

"Who?"

"Don't ask me who! I know you know what is going on. Please, tell me."

"Emma," he whispers, words lost in the storm. He

reaches for my cheek, but I pull back, unwilling to give him what he wants when he can't even answer my questions.

He looks hurt and understanding at the same time. Before I can stop him, Edgar pulls me into his arms. I struggle to get free, unwilling to accept his comfort.

"I'm sorry," he whispers into my ear. A sharp prick in my neck startles me, then I know no more.

CHAPTER TWENTY-SEVEN

Murder from the Heart

I mages of the knife flashing down and the stench of
garbage overwhelm my senses. I scream, but nothing
stops my attacker. I wake with a start, but I can't move.
With a moan, I try to open my eyes. My head is throbbing. It
feels like the world is spinning in circles. I think I might be
sick.

Voices ooze into my awakening senses, but I can't make
anything out just yet. I feel something hard beneath me, and
I can't move my arms or legs, no matter how much I try to.
My mind starts to clear.

"I can't do it. You know I can't. That's why I brought her
here."

"You have no choice!"

"It was your people who escalated this before I was
ready!"

"Maybe it needed to be escalated to stop you from
stalling so much and make you do what is needed."

A whimper pulls my attention from the argument I can
barely make out. Slowly, I force my eyes to open. The only
word I have is white. White walls and ceiling surround me. I
turn my head, eyes widening.

Gertrude is bound in the corner of this too-bright room.
Her eyes are wide, and she's covered in fresh cuts and
bruises. A few fingers are broken, resting at odd angles.
What is left of her disheveled bun looks sticky and stiff.

Those dark eyes hold an expression of pure desperation. She doesn't even notice me. I follow her gaze to the two men arguing in the corner.

Golden-brown eyes glare into golden-brown eyes. Edgar stares at Master Radcliffe, angry and seething. Master Radcliffe looks amused by his reaction.

"As you can see," my employer rasps calmly, "my people are being taken care of."

I notice the gesture toward Gertrude but don't follow it. I already saw her sorry state and have no desire to look upon it again. I should be elated to see her punished for what she has done to me, but instead, I only feel sorry for her. I can't hurt her, but it seems Master Radcliffe can.

"I am not ready," Edgar growls.

Master Radcliffe chuckles. "If it was left up to you, you would never be ready. It is what it is."

Edgar sighs and slumps in defeat. "It's her."

"Of course it is," the older man scoffs. "You knew it before I did, but I still didn't take long to figure it out. She's come home."

What? Who's come home? I struggle, finding out my wrists and ankles are strapped to a table that feels made of cold metal. This can't be good. I try to free myself again, but it is no use.

Edgar turns to me. "I'm sorry, dear Emma. There was nothing else I could do."

"What do you mean?" I question in a hoarse whisper. "Edgar, please, let me go."

"It has to be you." Master Radcliffe has not even looked my way.

Edgar's eyes snap back to him. "I cannot do it."

"Let me in," my employer replies. "I can, but it must be your hand."

"Never."

Master Radcliffe sighs. "We are going to go nowhere this way. If I do it, you know exactly what will happen. It needs to be done out of love, an emotion I no longer possess."

Hands trembling, Edgar nods with a deep breath. "For this reason only will I give you permission."

Laughter answers his words. "You know this will not be temporary, dear boy."

Edgar flinches with a nod. The old man places his hands on the younger's shoulders. In a flash of light, he is gone, leaving only Edgar in the room with me and my former supervisor.

"Please," I whisper, terrified of what is to come and not understanding anything.

Edgar picks up a large knife, and I tremble as the bright light gleams of the sharp blade. "I'm so sorry, Emma. This needs to be done. You will understand soon."

He turns to me, and my breath stops. I can still see warmness and regret in his golden-brown eyes, but there is a new coldness as well, one that I have seen in another set of eyes of the same color. Edgar lifts the knife above his head, and I scream and plead. I see him falter, but the coldness takes over. My screams peak as the blade slides into my chest and through my heart.

CHAPTER TWENTY-EIGHT

Completed Dreams

I am lost in the pages of my favorite book. It was years ago that I found this hidden treasure in the library, and I have yet to find the willpower to put it down. Waiting for my evening companion, I find it easier to pass the time with my nose stuck in this book. It is riveting.

"Again, Amelia?"

I smile and look up at the man I have been waiting for. "It took you so long!"

Golden-brown eyes smile down at me. "Sorry. My parents decided I needed to sit in on the whole meeting with the townspeople. Grooming me for when it is my turn to step up I guess."

"I don't know how you do it. I certainly wouldn't want the job."

My eyes drift back to the page.

"Seriously?"

One would think he's upset, but there's laughter in his voice. "I'm sorry, Edgar. I'll put the book down."

He walks over, grabs the book, and slides it into my purse. My eyes widen. "Your parents won't be upset."

My date laughs. "They won't even notice it's missing. If they do, they won't have a problem with me giving it to you. I thought you didn't like romance?"

"I don't normally, but this one has the perfect blend of mystery and adventure mixed within the sappy moments."

Edgar shakes his head and grabs my hand. "The book is not why you are here."

Following Edgar to the door, I take one last look around the bright library. Having access to so many different books must be so wonderful. A glance out the large windows of the library shows a bright sunset. It's so beautiful.

I'm led to the billiard room, and I can't suppress a giggle. "You aren't embarrassed to continue being beaten by a woman?"

"Maybe my luck has changed today."

I am sure he can see the challenge in my grin. "It is not luck. I just have skill."

He chuckles. "You never even played until I showed you how a few weeks ago."

"What can I say? I'm a natural."

Edgar closes the heavy tan drapes, so the only light in the room is the one illuminating the table. He lights a fire in the fireplace, and we spend most of the night hitting the balls around the table. Edgar's luck has not improved, and I continue to giggle as he tries to distract me to gain an advantage. The distraction doesn't work, and I remain undefeated.

"One more," I beg.

"We should get to dinner," he reasons. "I paid Peter to cook for us again because I know you love his cooking. By the way your face lights up, I can tell you are pleased."

"You really know how to talk a girl into eating."

He slips his arm through mine and walks me down the hall. "I thought food was the way to a man's heart, not a woman's."

I smile and drag him faster to the dining room. "The people who have said that have not eaten Peter's food. Are your parents joining us?"

Edgar shakes his head. "They want to give us privacy. I think they're hoping our relationship grows quickly."

"Yeah, sure," I say with a laugh.

The handsome man beside me grabs my hand and twirls me into an elegant spin right in the bright hallway. I laugh as my head flies back and the bright chandelier spins in my vision. When the twirl ends, I end up against Edgar, my hands pinned between our chests.

He smiles. "No one in this town can resist your charm."

"Aren't you a sweet talker?"

Instead of answering, Edgar leans in to give me a soft kiss on the lips. Despite how improper it is to be kissing in the middle of his parents' hall, I lean into it with my eyes closed. I can't deny this man anything. We stare into each other's eyes for a long time when the kiss is done.

He leans in for another, but I pull away with a laugh. "I'm hungry!"

My usual spot to his right is made ready for me. After holding out my chair, he takes his place at the end of the table. Peter brings us a wonderful meal, and I devour it in a very unladylike manner, to Edgar's amusement.

I squeal in delight when I realize that our dessert is to be one of the tear-shaped, chocolate-covered pastries that Mrs. Jones has just started baking. She tells me they don't have a name yet, but she'll let me know when she comes up with the perfect one.

After devouring my delicious pastry, I sigh and look up at the brightly lit chandelier. The windows show only darkness, but I cannot stop my sigh of contentment. When I look back at Edgar, he laughs and reaches over with a napkin. After dabbing chocolate from my lips, we sit and talk for a little while.

This man's company brings me nothing but comfort,

and I'm so glad to have found him. It's not like there are a lot of people in this town. That didn't stop the worry about whether or not I would find someone.

I look around the bright room and marvel at the richness showcased everywhere. Riches never interested me, but I love this place. Edgar's parents are basically in charge of the town. They use that power for good by keeping the buildings repaired and giving back to the people. No one minds.

Edgar asks me what I'm thinking. I smile. "I love how bright and airy it is here."

His eyes turn solemn. "My parents love to flood the place with light, but it was still a lonely childhood within these walls. You brought the brightness with you, Amelia. This place would be plunged into darkness without you."

My smile falls at the seriousness of his tone, and I touch his cheek. "Oh, Edgar. You don't need to worry about that. I won't ever leave you, and if anything did happen, I'd fight my way to get back to you. I love you."

A sad smile graces his lips. "I love you too, Amelia. I plan to hold you to that promise."

"I wouldn't have promised you if I didn't mean to keep it. Although, I do need to be getting home. Angel needs to be fed and cuddled."

"You and that cat," he laughs. "I do believe she's a huge point of competition for me."

I smile. "She is, but you two get along well. I'm sure she doesn't mind sharing."

By the entrance, we wait for the newest servant to bring my light jacket to ward off the chill of the night air. A tight black bun bobs on the top of her head, and her face holds an emotionless expression.

"Who is that?" I ask when she is out of earshot.

"That's Gertrude," Edgar answers. "She is young, but my parents say she had a rough life and are trying to help her by giving her employment."

We exchange goodbyes, and I walk out into the night after denying Edgar's insistence to let him escort me. I don't know what he thinks is going to happen in this small town. I wave to Isaac when I see him. He stands up from helping his father clean up their mess in the yard and waves enthusiastically. His father is grooming him to take over his duties when he gets too old to do so. The young man always has a smile for me.

My walk through the town is uneventful. I stop to talk to many of the townsfolk and greet others across the street, taking the long way home to speak with the people that I love so much. I love this town and wouldn't want to live anywhere else.

I circle behind the shops and up to the house my parents left me when they passed. I walk up the steps leading to my front door, happy to be home. The perfect end to my wonderful night will be to curl up with my black cat and read a good book.

It's dark, but the stars shine bright enough to give me some light. The full moon helps the stars light up my blue door and light beige house. After a few minutes of searching through my pink cloth purse, I find my keys, their jingling echoing in the night air. The cat that holds them together was a gift from Edgar; I think of him every time I look at it.

Out of nowhere, a chill passes over me, and I feel like someone is watching from the shadows. Goosebumps cover my skin. Angel meows from the window by the door, and I try to tell myself that she's the one watching me. Something deep inside tells me I'm wrong.

My key misses the hole in the doorknob as my hands

shake, scraping across the metal. I have always hated that sound. Footsteps echo, and I turn with a gasp. I know this man. What is he doing here?

Something metallic shimmers in the light of the full moon. The intent visible in his eyes makes me open my mouth to scream, but his gloved hand covers my mouth. I try to scream again. All I succeed in doing is making my lungs hurt.

Pain takes my breath away as he stabs my stomach. I am not sure how, but I manage to break away and make a run for it. I try to lose him by running down the alley, hand attempting desperately to hold the blood in my bleeding wound. A brief thought of the dress Edgar had given me being ruined by the blood runs through my mind, but I trip and fall by the smelly town dumpster, dispelling any other thought from my mind.

My attacker is on me, and I can feel the rough ground scrape my palms. I roll over and look up in terror. "Why are you doing this? Please, don't kill me."

The only answer I receive is the knife thrusting in and out of me. My screams echo around us, but I have no more strength to fight. My body begins to numb. The attacker runs off.

I hear someone screaming my name and see Edgar come into sight. He must've come to town for some late-night errands for his parents and wanted to check on me. Edgar is such a sweet man.

"Edgar," I whisper as the darkness takes over.

EPILOGUE

With a scream, I sit up, fighting the thick blankets holding me down. A richly furnished room surrounds the enormous bed I wake up in. My surroundings are unfamiliar, and I become confused. I try to think back on how I ended up here.

As memories of the white room come back to me, I cry out and clutch my hand over my heart. I peek inside the shirt I am wearing, only to find unblemished skin beneath. Even my arm feels better. Was it all a dream after all? This doesn't look like any hospital room I've ever seen.

My vision landed on the man who shoved a knife through my heart. My murderer sits on a chair at the foot of the bed, watching me with his golden-brown eyes. Those eyes trigger memories of the dream I just had, and my own widen in disbelief. What was that?

"Amelia...." Edgar breathes that word, eyes never leaving me.

"I'm not Amelia," I explain. "What did you do to me?"

He sighs, tilting his head back to stare at the ceiling. I take this time to look around. This room is brighter than the rooms I have seen throughout my stay here. The lamps throughout the room shine brilliantly, illuminating bright furniture and carpets. Even the drapes are thrown wide to let in brightness from outside. I feel like I'm in another world.

"I know you aren't her." My attention refocuses on the man at the foot of my bed. "At least, not completely, but she is still part of you. I can see it in your smile and hear it in your giggle."

"Why did you kill me?" As soon as the words exit my mouth, I open my eyes wider. Did I just accuse him of killing me, even though I'm sitting here without a scratch? Nothing makes any sense. I press the heels of my hands into my eyes to try to think.

"It had to be me. Any other way would have seen you lost in the hopelessness of the others murdered within this town. You would wander but be stuck in deep torment and unable to leave."

My hands fall to my lap. He just admitted to murdering me. "None of this makes any sense," I whisper before I can stop myself.

Edgar stares at me for a few moments before taking a deep breath. "Your dreams about your death aren't actually dreams. They are memories. I knew who you were the first day I met you, but I didn't believe it completely. It wasn't until you cried to me about your dreams that day on the road out of town that I could no longer deny it. I didn't see it happen, but I was there after. What you described brings back terrible memories."

He stops and looks at me with expectation, but I only stare for a few moments before saying, "That doesn't really clear it up for me, Edgar."

Edgar stands and begins to pace. "I had just spent the evening with her, and my parents wanted me to run something to the seamstress for repairs. I was on my way out when I heard a woman screaming. I found Amelia in the alley beside her home, covered in blood and dying in agony. Her last word was my name, and I have never gotten over that."

All warmth leaves my body. My last dream gains more

clarity. I remember the date and him calling me Amelia. I remember him running up to me as I lay dying on the cold ground. I remember all of it. "Still not making sense..."

Panic begins to course through me, and I search for a way to escape from this surreal reality he is telling me. Edgar takes a step closer to me, but Angel jumps on the bed. He stops and watches as the black cat rubs against me and purrs, happy to be by my side.

"She's missed you too," he tells me.

"But I'm not—"

"You are, in a way, which is why the town wouldn't let you leave. Your soul belongs here. Just let me explain before judging me. I'm not sure you will believe me."

I stare at him in disbelief. "Since I got here, I have been stalked by ghosts, freaked out by my employer, seen unexplainable things, almost been killed by my supervisor, driven to the brink of insanity, and killed by a man I thought I was falling for. Why don't you try me?"

Edgar freezes, his golden-brown eyes watching me in thought, then starts pacing again. "I was drowning in sorrow and grief. Amelia had been everything to me. My parents couldn't stop my spiral into darkness. The whole town grieved, but finding the culprit was proving difficult."

He pauses, continuing to pace. After a few breaths, he moves on. "I used every single resource I had to chase down the man who took the brightness from my world. Eventually, I was able to find him and..."

"And what?" I say after he remains silent too long. "You killed him?"

Edgar throws himself back into the chair, face buried in his hands. When he continues, his voice is no longer steady. "I did, and I enjoyed it. I found out that the man was upset with my parents over some judgment involving his business.

To hurt them, he decided to hurt me in the worst way possible. It was no secret how I felt about Amelia. That's when this part of me died and became trapped here."

"What do you mean this part of you died?" I let all the confusion I feel flow from my words, but he no longer answers.

After the silence stretches too long, I realize recounting all this may be too much for him. With plans to revisit the subject, I try to lead him away from his pain. "Who is Master Radcliffe? Is he your father?"

This would make sense to me. If something his father did caused Amelia's death, the anger against him would be justified. By the laughter coming from the broken man sharing the room with me, I guess that I'm wrong.

"That is a huge no, Emma." After a deep breath, he decides now is a good time to blow my mind. "Master Radcliffe is me, and I am him."

"That doesn't make any sense," I exclaim, ready to fly into a world of panic again until Angel meows and purrs, bringing me back to sanity. "I've seen you both at the same time. There is a darkness in his eyes that I have never seen in yours. He is also much older. You cannot be him."

Edgar examines his hands. "Remember when I told you that this part of me died with Amelia's murderer?"

I nod.

"Well," he continues, "it only killed this part of me. The darker part remained, only wanting to deal in violence in return for the shattered heart left within our chest. I became a whole different person, and my parents passed away shortly after, leaving that monster in charge.

"His rage and grief took over the town, creating a new hell for all those within. Since this part of me had already died, I could do nothing to stop him. The evil that overtook the town created some sort of barrier. People began to turn up dead, tortured in the worst ways possible. Younger people and children started to move away before the pull of the place got too strong. Those that died here never left. Eventually, everyone here was dead and trapped in this hell, including the kinder and gentler side of me."

I have no words to reply with. My mouth remains hanging open, and the rest of me is paralyzed. Disbelief must be apparent on my face as Edgar says, "You will understand more in time. You have to live it to truly understand."

"I-I- why did you kill me?"

Edgar rubs his eyes. "Amelia loved this town and people. I knew she would never be able to stay away from them, or me. She promised me. It was only a matter of waiting for her beautiful soul to return. You finally did."

"Does that mean the town is free?"

He laughs. "Unfortunately, no. The longer the town was stuck in this timeless place, the stronger whatever evil containing it became. It is no longer connected to Master Radcliffe or myself."

"What happened to Master Radcliffe?"

Edgar looks at me. The warmness disappears, replaced by a familiar coldness for a few seconds. "We are one once again. There was no way I could have done what was needed without him. That's one of the reasons I pulled away from you. I wasn't hurt, not completely. I wished you could run away. I just knew I couldn't do what needed to be done. Only by becoming one with the monster side of me was I able to save you from the fate of those women who came before you."

"Will he continue to hurt the town?"

Edgar sighs and stands, heading to the door. "That will depend on you. He is as happy as me that you are back,

Emma; in whatever form. If he feels that you are not trying to do what he sees as your duty to be Amelia again, I don't think I can contain him. He will never hurt you, but the town will suffer his anger. They may all have died, but he can still make them feel pain. He quite enjoys it."

I have no response as he walks from the room. Gertrude enters after his exit, and I jump to my feet. She rolls her dark eyes. "Relax. What good would it do for me to try to hurt you now?"

Gertrude hangs the black bag on the hook of the door I assume to be the closet. "The young master requests your presence at dinner tonight. This dress has been delivered for you. Try not to keep him waiting, mistress."

When she leaves, I stand and walk over to the bag, then unzip it to reveal a familiar turquoise dress with the braided black belt. It's finished and waiting for me, but I feel a little uncomfortable. Edgar's words about keeping the master happy echo within my head. Even though none of this makes any sense, I have encountered too much to not believe. I slip the dress on.

I enter the dining room to see Edgar sitting at the end, right where Master Radcliffe used to sit. The younger man stands and pulls out a seat at my entrance. The place I have been setting for no one seems to be my own. I chew on my lip a bit, but hurry over and sit when Edgar raises an eyebrow.

I have a part to play.

ALSO AVAILABLE

Bìtan
—

Chapter 1: Monsters

The bright light of the moon beats back the shadows of the forest, which brings me back to memories of my mother telling me monsters don't exist. Not in the shadows, under my bed, or anywhere else. She is wrong, and I never understood how she missed the one right in front of us. Maybe she was used to the monster, but I could never become accustomed to him.

Looking up at the moon, I feel a chill run through me, filling me with a sense of foreboding that halts the sound of my pencil scratching against paper. What if we are both wrong? The shadows cast by the moon may hide anything from the naked eye. Goosebumps cover my flesh as I sense someone watching me. After convincing myself that I'm letting my mind play tricks, I laugh and remind myself that the only monsters in this world are evil human beings.

With a quick shake of my head, I dispel my irrational

thoughts and go back to shading the orb I'm drawing over the wolf's head I sketched on the way here. Drawing has always been my favorite way to channel my creativity. Everyone tells me I should do this for a living. I'm afraid drawing for money would suck the love I have for it away.

I use the resumed scratching of my pencil to drown out the sounds of my friends eating each other's faces across the fire. I'm not even sure how they both managed to fit in that camping chair. Underestimating their ability to make out in the weirdest places is another talent of mine. It seems I have many.

"Hey there, Red Riding Hood. Do you ever draw anything else?" Jim's breath fans my neck as he looks over my shoulder.

"What's wrong with wolves?" In my opinion, nothing. I love wolves. They're gorgeous animals that make beautiful music. How can someone not like wolves? That's the real question.

Jim plops down in the chair next to mine, placing his ice-cold beer in the built-in cupholder and handing me the soda I asked for. Alcohol makes me nervous with my family's history. They can drink all they like, but I refuse. "Nothing. It's just all you draw."

"I draw other things."

He laughs. "Sure you do."

"Also," I say to change the subject, "I told you that nickname doesn't fit me."

"Oh, it so does. You always wear that red hoodie, and you love wolves. It's perfect."

Giving up on my sketch, I put my drawing pencil back in its case. "I'm pretty sure Little Red Riding Hood didn't love wolves. They ate her grandma."

"Details..."

"Why does Julia get a normal nickname?"

Jim looks at me as if I grew an extra head. "Her name may be Julia, but I call her Jules because she likes jewelry, not because of her name."

"And Skippy?"

"He skipped two grades, duh."

I laugh, closing my sketchbook. "What are we, back in high school?"

"Just because you're twenty-five doesn't mean you have to act like you're ninety. Live a little, Red."

I sigh. "Where *are* Julia and Andrew?"

"Andrew is such a boring name."

"Okay... Jules and Skippy..."

"That's better," he sighs, stretching his feet out toward the crackling fire. "They went in search of more wood."

"That was a while ago."

Jim laces his fingers behind his head and leans back. "You know them. They're probably going at it in front of a bear or something."

I snort, turning my head away to try to hide it. "Let's change the subject, please."

"Fine. About next weekend. I think we should go visit your parents."

"Any subject but that. Where did you leave the lantern?"

Jim points at the tent we share, and I see the green canvas glowing with the light within. "I left it in there so we can make shadow puppets when we go to bed."

He wiggles his eyebrows up and down. My cheeks become hotter than the fire in front of us. "Oh my god!"

My embarrassment makes him laugh. "Stop changing the subject. You need to forgive. At least your mother. Your dad can go to hell."

"She isn't blameless. She let it happen. Enabling is just

as bad. I liked the shadow puppet subject better, Jim. Can we go back to that?"

"I bet you did," he winks. "Wait until you see my talent later. By the way, don't call me Jim, Little Red Riding Hood."

"I am not using the nickname you gave yourself!"

"Do it! I'll show you why I deserve it later."

"Fine, my big bad wolf."

He leans in for a kiss that never reaches completion. Our friends scream as a streak of black slams into their chair. I jump to my feet, Jim stepping in front of me. Looking over his shoulder, I see a big black wolf with red eyes rip the arm off Jim's older brother in one bite. My hands grip my boyfriend's shirt until my knuckles hurt.

The girlfriend has fallen into the fire. She somehow manages to pull herself out and roll on the ground while screaming. As soon as the flames are out, the wolf is on her. She tries to hold him off as he goes for her throat, the blisters on her arms glowing in the firelight.

Jim drags me over to my tent and shoves me in it. "Close the flap!"

"I'm not leaving you out there!"

"Just do—"

A strangled scream cuts my boyfriend's words off as he's pulled back. I grab his hands, but it's no use. I cannot pull him from the beast's jaws. Blood sprays as he is pulled toward the fire. I stare, frozen as the warm liquid rolls down my face.

When I see the beast open Jim's belly, I throw up the snacks I ate earlier and close the flap. Clothes, shoes, and books fly across the tent as I look for any kind of weapon, anything I can use to save myself. I can hear the wolf clawing at my tent door. My time is limited.

When I hear canvas tear, I grab the lantern and swing it.

The wolf yelps when steel connects with his nose, but he doesn't slow. Agonizing pain sears through my ankle as sharp teeth clamp down. I can feel bones crunch, forcing a blood-curdling scream from my mouth.

My yells of pain mix with sobs as the wolf drags me from the tent by my ravaged ankle. Next thing I know, his jaws are coming for my face. When I try to block him, the bones in my wrist are crushed. I'm crying and begging for my life as my blood mixes with Jim's on my face.

I try to roll to avoid the next lunge of those vicious fangs. The wolf misses my neck but bites into my right shoulder instead. Screams of agony surprise me with the level they reach. I never thought I'd ever hear such brutal sounds come from myself, not after all the pain I've dealt with in the past. This is a whole different level.

A different cry echoes in the air, followed by the clattering of wood. I watch as Andrew tries to drag the beast off Julia. Her unseeing eyes fall on me, half her jaw missing. I turn from the carnage, finding my sketchbook open to the drawing I've been working on.

Blood covers my sketch of the moon as my vision begins to darken. The wolf growls and snarls before a loud bang shatters the air around the ravaged campsite. Sweet unconsciousness starts to consume me, the world growing dark to hide the surrounding carnage.

I guess monsters are real, after all.

ABOUT THE AUTHOR

Jessie Roberts can be contacted at jessierobertsbooks@ gmail.com

<u>Follow the Author</u>

For more information on Jessie Roberts and upcoming titles, please visit: